Grendel's Mother

Diana Stout

Cover design by Cover Bistro
Formatting by Sharpened Pencils Productions LLC
(Corrected Edition May 2024)

ISBN 10: 0-9974223-0-0
ISBN-13: 978-0-9974223-0-6

DEDICATION

To Dr. Jana Schulman, whose question of *Was Grendel's Mother human or monster?* solidified my own question. And to Penny Kelly, who recognized the true reality of this book long before I did.

CONTENTS

ACKNOWLEDGMENTS

Many thanks to my fans and readers, with a special thank you for those of you who leave reviews. I am most grateful.

You've made me want to be a better writer and an even better editor.

GRENDEL'S MOTHER

History becomes legend and legend becomes myth.
Lord of the Ring / Fellowship

All journeys begin with a single step. I could say my journey began when I was made dead, a no-name ghost in the woods. Or, when I first met the dragon when I was too young to be afraid. Or, maybe my journey began when the pains started, soon after the last thread of light disappeared in a horizontal sliver crushed between dark ominous clouds fast filling the sky and the earthly boundaries of both my chains and comfort as deemed by the gods: the raw wilderness. Was it only less than a year ago that I was a naïve child, believing that the life ahead of me was mine to choose? So innocent. So lost in my own little world of supposed freedom. Self-centered as only a child knows at the time. What a difference a year makes.

At the moment, I am working within my wilderness, attempting to catch a wild pig. The temperature has dropped, with late, major winter storm clouds moving in too quickly. I need major sustenance for the next couple days, if not weeks, and this yearling can satisfy that need. My spear is ready. I hold my breath, waiting. Now, all I need is for the pig to turn parallel to me, so that I have a broader target, where I can hit a major organ.

I'm cold and don't relish hunting in the dark, but I have no choice.

I let go of my discomfort. Up until now, I've been able to ignore the pains, the tightening of my mid-section. Thankfully, the clouds aren't covering the full moon high in the sky . . . yet. The moon provides enough light for me to hunt. My hands, face, and any other exposed skin are blackened with mud, and I wear enough fur that I smell like the forest and the animals within.

The pig turns. I throw my spear. It hits right where I aimed—its heart. It squeals loudly, takes a couple steps, and drops. I get up from my kneeling position, where I was hidden in the tall grass, moving far slower than I want. My huge belly makes me awkward and slower than I like. I gasp as my belly tightens again. Mentally, I count. Finally, the muscles relax. I need to hurry.

Nearly at the pig, I walk around it so that its back is to me, just in case it is still alive. If it were to get up, it would not be facing me. I grab the top of the spear that stands straight up to the sky and wiggle it, so I can see the belly . . . a female. She's dead.

Good. I don't want to have to stab her again. Slowly, I drop to my knees and pull out my knife. In just a few minutes, I have her disemboweled, dressed as much as I can perform in the shortest of time. The dressing is sloppy compared to my usual precise cuts, but I don't care. Time is my priority, right now. I am initially saddened to discover she's pregnant, but the reality is that it is either her or me; otherwise, I'd have no food for the next couple of weeks. Normally, when I see a pregnant pig, I leave her alone, to live another day, but there wasn't any sign she was pregnant. The piglets are barely formed. Normally, I would take the whole pig back to the cave and gut it there. Nothing is ever wasted. Today isn't a normal day, though. I need to get back to the cave quickly and I can't carry a whole pig with its innards today. I stand up and gasp.

The realization of what is happening hits me hard. When did I allow this child to enslave my future? To reduce me to hunting in the freezing cold like this, to put all my creature comforts aside? That's a laugh. When was the last time I had a real creature comfort? When I suckled at my mother's breast, perhaps?

Another pain clenches my middle, creating a new kind of tightness. I make myself breathe through the pain, having nothing to lean on, to grab hold of. The spear lies on the ground. Finally, the pain lessens. I retrieve the spear and walk over to the nearest tree, leaning the spear against the trunk. I retrace my steps, bending over as best I can, grabbing the pig's hind legs. I lift her over my shoulder awkwardly, not liking that I can't maneuver her around my neck as I would have done normally. I do the best I can.

I grab the spear and head for the cave. Far too soon, I feel the burning in my back and shoulder muscles begin. Fortunately, I'm not far from my destination.

There was a time when I thought I had been one with the earth. A time when I had honored the seasons by tradition. How little I knew back then. How young I was. My time with Nature then had been equal to tiptoeing across a room, minimum and shallow, with little effort.

It wasn't until I was forced from everything I knew, by the hand of my father and mother who didn't object in any way to my ostracization and execution, that I became one with Nature.

In truth, my journey began much earlier, an earlier day and its night, when my world was turned upside down. As the only girl in a large household of boys and a wee baby sister who lived only a few days, I learned my mother's skills, both inside the house and outside in the gardens.

The herbal garden was all about magick. Her magick. As a young girl, I was determined that one day it would be mine, as well. Women sought ma's healing knowledge. It wasn't unusual for these women to travel a long day's journey for ma's ability to make unwanted births disappear, with no one the wiser except ma and me. I grew up in that garden, crawling between plants, tasting which were bitter, which were sweet, and which were poison, earning me a resounding slap from ma before I could poison myself. I hid among the tomato plants, thick with green, both in leaf, stalk, and fruit. I watched the bugs, butterflies, and worms, learning which plants they avoided and those they devoured. Nature revived me. I was in awe of all its mysteries and secrets. I hated being stuck in the house, with its dark, cave-like features. With no windows, once the door was shut, only firelight enabled one to see.

I never minded the dirt, whether it was garden, forest, or meadow, though da kept telling ma she'd have to clean me up if there was to be a good match. I wasn't interested in a match. I was interested in being free to roam the land, to experience its smells, its life that bore fruit with plants and flowers galore. To be stuck in the house with those awful chores was like prison. Could there be any worse punishment?

Household skills came to ma easily, too easily—skills that every young woman requires to be worthy of a husband and to raise a family. Next to her, I moved like an ox—so she said—despite the fact I was quick on my feet . . . when I had to be. If I wasn't quick, I often caught the back of her hand or my brothers' pinches. But unknown to ma and da, I had skills no one was aware of. Man skills. True, they were unpracticed skills because I was still learning, but given time, one day I would be as sought after as ma.

Raised in a household of boys, I was curious and eager to learn the other skills that swirled around me in conversation: hunting, trapping, creating goods from leather, weapons, combat, farming, livestock, and more. To my way of thinking, having knowledge was more important than perfecting the skill, especially since that knowledge was forbidden me. I should think a husband would want me to have those skills, allowing me to be a true helpmate. Though, I imagine da would box my ears if he ever heard me expressing that idea aloud. He believes women are only good for three things: rutting, birthing sons, and putting food on the table, and not necessarily in that order.

With the swoop of one devastating event followed by another delivered unexpectedly and swiftly, however, everything changed.

Now, I am the seasons: Nature and I are one. Though She is my shackle that separates me from civilization, strangely I am free. She nourishes me. I forage Her rich bounty to fill my stomach, shelter dry in Her cavern rock and earth, and find warmth within Her furs from those who sacrifice their lives so that I might live. She fills my mind and enriches me in ways no man ever could or can.

Never again will any man claim me as his.

To anyone who knew me in my other life, my name is forgotten, gone, eradicated from lips and minds alike, the result of the village decree. To them, I no longer exist.

I am dead.

Despite that dreadful day where this baby was forced into me, despite that decree, despite the so-called people who claimed to have loved me, yet sent me to my death so easily, I am very much alive.

The pains remind me just how alive I am and the life I am about to give. The thing I fear most, the only future I have now and also a reminder of the past and the event that ruined my once idyllic and happy life, coalesces into the round belly that tightens harder, this time catching me off guard.

Instinctively, I catch my breath. I try to relax. The night will be long, and I will be exhausted by night's end, for my work has only begun. Finally, I'm at the mere's edge. Quickly, I drop the pig and strip, hiding the only piece of clothing I wear, a fur robe, placing it out of sight but where it will remain dry.

I grab the pig's hind legs again. Taking a deep breath, I jump into the water, the pig in one hand, the spear in the other. Rather than feeling fat and clumsy, now I am buoyant with better flexibility. Because I've performed this task multiple times, I don't have to think about it.

Quickly, I swim the distance, diving deep down, then beneath the rock, and then back up and into the cave, until I can feel the cave floor ledge under my feet. Fortunately, for me, this underwater ledge allows me to stand and toss the pig up onto the dry floor in front of me. I toss the spear forward and start climbing, eventually rolling onto the cave floor as my strength wanes.

My teeth clatter and I shiver. I grab a fur and start rubbing myself dry. Another contraction stops me, forcing me to wait and endure its presence. The contractions are getting longer and more intense.

I want to call out, but I can't just in case anyone could hear my cry. Sound carries more easily in the winter where there are no leaves and bushes outside to buffer the noise. I have to hurry.

Unlike that time of the past when I helped babes into the world, never far from my mother's side, learning from her vast experience and coaxing soft words that she had for the wee ones, there is no such person here to help me. The dragon has mentored me as much as she can for this event. Now, she sleeps. The only time she isn't sleeping is when she's out hunting for food, which isn't often. Her life experience in giving birth is nonexistent, but her wisdom is Universal. She says the infant will have great strength because its birth will be a solitary event. All the spirits and energy will gather and flow into the child rather than being dispersed by the spiritually destructive presence of midwives, curious women, excited children, and fathers demanding sons. For the moment, there is no comfort other than my own words and thoughts. While I don't like how the past dominates my thinking, to reserve the energy that I will need later, I give up control.

My mind wanders as I methodically cut off a hock, skewer it on a sharpened stick and then place it on a spit over the fire. Now, I wish I still had an organ or two, especially the heart or liver. I've learned to eat these raw while the blood is still warm. I always feel energized, almost as if I've embraced and enveloped the energy of the creature.

Too tired to cut up the meat and smoke it, I store it instead. Moving toward a big rock at the back, I move a large slab of rock that acts like a door, revealing a natural hollow in the rock that for some reason is far cooler than the rest of the cave with the slab in place. The meat will stay cool and protected from most all predators. I'm careful not to touch any of the spider webs nearby as they help keep the smallest of prey—the pesky fly—from finding the meat.

I reach for some clothes, then change my mind. I won't need clothes tonight. A tanned skin—one of my first—that serves as a blanket will suffice. Tired to the core, I sink down on the skins. A contraction comes and goes. Several more follow.

The low fire, rich with coals, creates shadows that flicker on the cave's limestone walls, and like stars in the sky, dots of light showcase minerals throughout the rocky walls.

High on the wall in front of me, on a narrow rock shelf, lies a sizeable and once shiny sword, a prize the dragon claimed long before I took lodging here. She keeps the sword as a reminder of how evil man can be, having told me the tale of the man who hatched and raised her after finding an egg tucked beneath a slain dragon with nearly a hundred arrows in its chest. Just as she started to become too big to stay hidden in the forest behind the man's village, she chanced upon a conversation between the farmer and the village leaders. She hadn't been a secret at all. The man's intent, the village's intent was to offer her as a sacrifice against the evil spirits of a poor harvest, a ceremony to take place in another few months when they believed she would start breathing fire. What the man didn't know was that she had been spitting fire and flying for several weeks. Although she wasn't fully practiced in either, she made it her mission to be gone by day's end. Hearing that she was to be slain by the magical sword stolen from the king's treasury, now hidden in the forest, high in a hollow of the great oak tree that stood near the mouth of the small hillside cave where she rested at night, she retrieved the sword and left that night under the cover of darkness. Well hidden in this cave, she laid the sword high on a natural shelf, out of reach and sight from man's temptation should the cave be found. Only the tallest of men would be able to see it, and even then, he would need to be in the right spot in the cave to notice it.

While I have a desire to eliminate all potential connections to men and their kind, I have no desire to remove the sword from its perch. I respect the dragon too much to tamper with what little she claims as hers. So, I ignore the sword and hope that in years to come, as the dust builds, it will disappear from sight, fading into the background.

As I focus on the cave walls, my home for the past seven months, I feel as if I've been here for years. When I first entered this place, I was starving, cold, and uncertain that I would survive, let alone bring a new life into the world. Was it only months ago when I dove into the cold mere and mistakenly found my way into this hidden cave? In time, I made this a home, my home, and became quite possessive when other creatures of the forest, other than the dragon, tried to make it theirs. Now, their furs are beneath me or stacked nearby.

I welcomed the dragon because there was a time that she had been my protector, rescuing me from death. How could I turn her away when she was in need, tracked down by men determined to slay her? She remains deep in the cave, in a different room, far from sound and view, coming and going from an opening that is unknown to me. She stays out of my way, and I hers.

The furs stacked to my right comfort me. Most need work; only a few are ready as bedding or clothing for the onslaught of winter that is as sure to come as the next contraction. There is still much to do if this child and I are to survive through the harshest of this last bit of the winter season.

At home, fir trees would have been cut and brought into the house in celebration of winter solstice, and then throughout the winter months, the pine scent would mask the otherwise stale and pungent odor that lingered heavily until spring when the doors were left open.

I feel lucky just to have anything that can burn, not caring how it smells. I realized when first alone on how my skills were lacking in deed compared to my ideas, and how I wished I had spent more time observing my brothers. Over time, though, I have learned.

To think of the past is only a reminder of how I was shunned, forgotten, my existence wiped away. Yet, I go there naturally, as if living in the past was a daily event rather than the battle I have waged for the last seven months not allowing myself to remember, to think of it, of them, of him.

At first, when cast aside, I was fearful. I'd been brave when living in my father's house, sneaking out at night, going into the forest that was my sanctuary. While I had a healthy fear of the attackers who streamed out of the forests from time to time, I was careful. Any fear I had for these attacking warriors was nothing compared to the all-consuming fear I initially felt, though, when I was thrown out of the community. Over time, the fear of those strangers became ghost-like compared to the initial days and weeks of isolation that followed my expulsion. Then, I had been fractured, but not anymore. Today, I welcome my aloneness. As a result of being alone with no one except for myself and the dragon's advice from time to time, I have become whole. While the dragon and I are kindred spirits alone in the wilderness, sharing a cave, we are unable to truly assist each other.

The morrow, though, will change my status. If I succeed in this delivery, I will be in company, no longer just one. If I should fail, I will be more alone than even I want to think about. It is because of this baby that I fought and continue my fight to live no matter the circumstances of his or her being.

Negative thoughts of the future are a curse for any birthing mother. The dangers of the night's journey are many. I try to change my focus away from such negative thoughts and find a bright spot of time, even if it is in the past that ultimately led to my destruction. A gripping pain, spanning from hip to hip, inches toward my back and leaves me breathless.

"Nooooooooooooooo," I cry out to those who no longer listen. The cave echoes my cry. The pool of water that dominates this room's mystical center ripples at the vibration, and the fire's reflection wavers. I do not fear waking the dragon. She slumbers heavily in her chamber, located many rooms and great lengths into the cave.

Another pain tightens my belly. You won't get the best of me, I tell the memories, but they are deaf to my words.

The past rises before me, easily, and without conscious effort. Reluctantly, I allow that time to surround me. I am too tired to stave those memories off any longer. I need to escape to that place and space for a brief time, for right now that painful past is nothing compared to the pain in my body. As a focal point, I want the past to anger me, as that anger will help me maintain my strength through the night. I grit my teeth. The tears I shed months ago were the last that I will shed for those whom I was forced to leave behind: my innocent younger siblings. Anyone else is guilty and should be ashamed of their sin. My mother more than anyone.

I spit on the ground in disgust as the pain rescinds, and then lean back on layers of moss, a pillow for my head. Thunder cracks overhead, but the sound here in my sheltering cave muffles the sound. I am safe from the weird winter storm that in my mind's eye pelts icy fingers of sleet across the landscape, frosting trees with a glistening sheen. A tempest of another kind swirls within my belly, reminding me of that other storm. The early storm . . . where my journey began on a clear, cloudless, early spring day.

* * *

"Girl! Where are you?"

I push the light brown strands of hair that have escaped the long braid away from my eyes, raise my head, and peer over the tops of the rows of onions, which I obediently weed and have been doing so for the past hour despite the exceptionally early debilitating heat and humidity for this time of year. I squint my eyes against the sun that is late-afternoon bright, directly in front of me, just above the roof of the cottage. My vision dims and I feel dizzy, but I ignore the symptoms and strain, focusing on the figure in the distance. With her arm in the air, my mother signals for me to come in from the garden. Not wanting to be free of this duty, I sigh, rising from my kneeling position, knowing full well that my release from this chore that I actually enjoy is only so that I can be assigned another one, no doubt more tedious.

Taller than ma and some of my brothers, reed-like, and determined like da and far more stubborn than ma, as the oldest daughter—the only daughter—the care of my younger six siblings often falls to me. I curse my three older brothers, envying their ability to be in the field with da. Even though their work is just as hard as mine, at least their mother isn't boring down on them at every turn.

I was born in the fall fifteen years ago when the winds begin to howl, announcing imminent snows. The only two redeeming features about my birth, according to my mother, is that the garden harvest was finished, and she was able to stay inside and rest more than usual after the birth. There were more women available to help tend to my brothers' care, keep the cottage clean, and cook meals for them and da. Plus, the fact that I was small and slid out easily. Having witnessed the birth of the six brothers and one sister who followed me, and having assisted in the arrival of the last four, I find many of the village women envy my mother. All her births were easy, and unlike many of the households where other women die, my mother thrives in her fertility.

The morning had been good. Ma and I had worked side by side in the garden, harvesting herbs she will need for the week for various ailments—a typical week in the village: bites, cuts, bruises, women's ailments, a leg or foot sliced open by an ax when chopping, and then the war wounds that occur from time to time as men fight to keep our village safe from marauders. These times we spend together, while not rare, are not frequent enough to suit me. I much enjoy the softer side of ma. However, the afternoon was even more pleasurable, as I found myself alone in the dirt and plants. It isn't often that I get to be alone this many hours without interruption.

Almost to the bare patch of ground that surrounds our cottage, I bend to the ground and snap a dandelion, my favorite of all flowers, from its long stem. I'm careful not to disturb the flower's seeds that are clustered in a ball. Once bright yellow like a new sun on the morning's horizon, the petals offer promise, more to the birds and insects than to me. Seeing these hardy flowers populate the fields always makes me smile. By night, stars dot the skies; by day, dandelions dot the landscape. Such a small innocuous plant, it holds the promise of continuance as it blooms throughout the summer, unlike the iris that produces a new blossom every day for only a couple weeks, or the tulip or crocus that herald in the spring and are gone as quickly as they come, or even the buttercup or lilies that are favorites among the women here in the village but are often as short-lived as these women. True, the dandelion is common and often ignored, as it is plentiful, hardy, and close to the ground. Often, the flower is spoiled by trampling feet, or is hidden by tall grasses, yet, it survives. It is the hardiest of all flowers.

At the back door, I stop and take a deep breath, my concentration on the flower. I hear the door creak open. I blow at the seeds. Only half of them detach and drift away, carried by the slightest of breeze. My mother steps out and brushes the air with agitated motion, then knocks the stem from my hand.

"Stupid, girl! How many times do I have to warn that you dance with death? Blow seeds away and it's the year you're doomed to die!"

"A superstition." I pass her and enter the house.

She follows me back into the house. "She bleeds a few months and suddenly an expert of the herbs and plants," she mutters to herself. Then to me, she says, "you have much to learn."

"So you say," I reply. The words are out before I consider what I am saying. She has that power over me, to get me to respond, and often, to my own dismay. I know better than to respond, and yet I do. I skirt around the table, out of her reach, on the pretense of wanting to finish the job she had obviously been busy with: tying bundles of herbs that will hang from the ceiling to dry. This time of year is when the house smells with new herb scents mingling, masking the long winter's stink—animals and humans confined together in closed quarters.

She chooses to pretend that I said nothing. "The dandelion holds death in its seeds. It's no superstition, not when my brother Neil died in battle the day after such a blow."

"They're seeds. Seeds that produce. You're the one who says that seeds are the lifeblood of our land."

"Those seeds produce death, I tell you, especially when blown. The greens may be good to eat but the flower is bitter poison to the future of anyone who plays with it. My brother is not the only one who died after tempting the dandelion's power."

She rambles and I let her, not listening. I'm hungry and want the herb tying finished so that I can clear the table for our final meal of the day. Being combative with her does no good. In the end, if she is angry enough, I'll still get the backside of her hand. According to her, it doesn't matter that every Dane who fought the south-invading Saxons that day died in battle. Had it not been for her brother blowing out a dandelion the day he left for battle, she says, he'd still be alive. Stupid superstitious woman.

The last of the bundles hung, I turn my attention and concentrate on the next chore, getting supper ready. It will be dark soon and the men will come in from the fields expecting food on the table. I hate how every day is the same, one following another, and how I, as a girl, have to serve the men and the boys first, before I can sit down and eat. Sometimes, there is barely a morsel or two left for me and ma to share. It isn't fair. I am just as strong as my brothers, nearly as tall as they, and I can do a day's work out in the field equally well. Wearing a skirt is a hindrance. How I wish I could wear britches, too.

Da and the brothers clomp heavily into the room, negligent in kicking the dried mud off their boots before crossing the threshold, uncaring that the mud falls off in clumps, then is stepped on by the one behind them. Quickly, the hard-packed dirt floor has paths soft and slick. I sigh.

Attempting to sweep food droppings after dinner that can later attract rats in the night will be near impossible. It would be nice not to have to sweep after every meal, to scrub dishes, or to help put the little ones to bed. I am weary just thinking about all the work yet to do, knowing that I was up early, well before the rest of the family so I could serve them breakfast. I know ma is just as weary, more so, and yet she always finds time to talk and giggle with da late into the night.

I often hear them as I lie on my pallet, waiting for the house to slumber so I can sneak out into the woods and breathe the night air, undisturbed, and under the stars. That time alone is the only real freedom I experience each day. I always move far enough away from the house where I can't be seen, but not so far away that I can't cry for help if needed. Travelers are known to lurk in the countryside, coming into communities to raid the pens and hen houses, but those crimes are diminished in comparison to the wars raging all around us and disease rumored to have its grip on the country again.

Most nights, I hear ma's giggles and da's low, rumbling voice.

Then ma sighs and moans intermittently before the strange sounds cease and all is quiet in the sequestered corner of the long house, the sleeping quarters. I am always amazed that the babies who sleep nearby never wake up during those times. I used to wonder what da was doing to her that made her moan so, until finally I asked one of my brothers, who simply pointed to the pasture where the sheep rutted. Ever since then, I try not to listen; yet, I still hear, even when I cover my face and ears with my blanket. Despite the moans, da's rutting must be pleasurable, in view of the number of moans I hear each week.

Considering the number of babies she's had, I never see ma push da away when he teases her, slapping her backside, not like other women who push their husbands away.

I watched the animals more closely after that and noticed how one female cat would prance back and forth before the toms, her tail twitching excitedly in the air. Then, she would plop down in front of one, with her hind end practically in his face. He would mount her, biting her neck. Then she would growl, barring her teeth to him, and he would move off quickly, taking a few steps away. Purring, she would then flip over to her backside with all four legs in the air. He would stand there looking at her as if perplexed. I wondered if he was puzzled as I was. Why growl and then purr?

I wanted to ask ma but was afraid to.

I remember ma and the other women talking last winter about one of the other young girls in the village and how she had lost favor with her family because she looked at the boys. She disappeared by the end of summer. Anytime I ask about her, ma ignores me. Da, hearing me ask, tells me to be quiet. After a time, I've learned not to ask at all, but I listen when others talk. I want to know what happened to her. I learn nothing, though. No one is saying. When they do say, they must be talking in code, as every now and then, I hear conversations that don't make sense. Until finally, one day, when ma and I were in the garden and she was having a good day, I learned that the girl had gotten pregnant and was given to a man from another village, along with two goats. Later she died, beaten by her new husband for birthing a girl.

The baby was said to have died, too, since there was no one to nurse her.

To da I am useless, nothing more than a servant to do his bidding. My brothers, follow his example. Once upon a time, when I was little, they treated me with kindness, but now they treat me as if I don't exist except to serve their needs: cook their food, clean up after them, and treat their injuries. I am continually disgusted by the separation of the sexes. Ma finds favor with the community leaders and da because she knows how to produce male heirs. "It's all about position and the herbs," I often hear her say. Other women covet her skills and knowledge of the wild fields and gardens. Her teas and remedies are sought after by the women. Some recipes she gives out; most she keeps hidden. I watch her closely whenever she mixes her secret recipes. Her patch of tended crops is beautiful; but more importantly, her garden is potent and magical.

The women ask about different plants, and while ma names them, she and I both know she doesn't provide the real name. I know that some of the more potent plants have come to her from her mother and grandmother, rare to find wild in the fields and forest. Nor do other women have her mixing knowledge. Her mortar and pestle are worn smooth from the wear of many generations of women having ground their secrets. While ma has been teaching me, I know more than she thinks. I watch her more closely than she realizes.

Anytime ma is in her garden, I follow her. It is the one place where I can ask a question and she answers willingly. She is loving, kind, and gentle when in her garden. Obviously, to share this knowledge is important; as the oldest girl in the family, I am the heir inherent. Men aren't given this kind of knowledge, she once told me years ago when as I was less obstinate and argumentative. "Men have enough power," she said. "They don't use it all or use it well. Knowledge of the fields and of Nature is our protection. Nature is our wisdom, our strength. It holds our power, but we have to be still and listen." And so, I listen and learn.

I experiment having created a pestle and mortar out of Nature's leftovers: a piece of wood, the size of my fist, which I hollowed out the bowl, too shallow for my liking, and a stout rock that is more barrel-like than a ball, with enough length that I can palm it easily like a stick but with a fat end that I could pummel the herbs, seeds, and flowers that I gather from ma's garden and in the wild. The cats are my subjects. I mix my concoctions in their food and then watch their reactions. So far, I've learned that wormwood burned in close quarters made a tomcat dizzy and then near death until I opened the shed's door.

One time, my older brother, Ewan, wouldn't leave me alone, so I put pokeweed in his porridge. He couldn't keep any food in his stomach for a couple days. And recently, I discovered that elder seeds are poisonous. I took the body of that cat, when no one was looking, deep into the woods where no one would find it.

"More food, girl," da says. I rise from my seat, having just sat down, and reach for the empty bowl that is in front of me. I go to the fire and ladle more stew into the bowl. I move toward da, to serve him, when I notice one of the cats in the shadows of the room walking lopsided, as if it has drunk too much ale. Earlier, I added just the tiniest bit of elder seed to its food. I wanted to find out if elder seed could induce sickness rather than death.

I bump into da. My fingers slip and the bowl tips toward him. Half of the hot contents splatter and spill on him before I can right the container.

Da growls from the pain, jumps up, his arm making a quick, wide arc that catches me on the side of the ribs, hard enough that my entire body rises in the air, and I fly several feet backward before falling to the ground. I hit the floor hard. Spears of pain shoot up my spine with excruciating pain. My head snaps back and my teeth clamp down on my tongue. My head hits a hard, immoveable object behind me. I taste blood, and my tailbone feels as if on fire. My head hurts from the jolt. Somehow, I managed to hang onto the bowl. While the bowl is in my lap, the remainder of the food that was in the bowl now covers my chest. The heat is nothing to the pain I feel in my mouth, my back, and my head.

"Stupid bitch!" He turns on ma and hits her. "What did you teach her?" Ma cowers in a way I've never seen before.

It is common for me to be the recipient of da's temper, but never ma. "Worthless women, the lot of you!" He stomps out of the house. I hear water splashing outside, back by the door where the bucket of wash water sits. Da is cooling the heat I brought to his arm.

Despite the pain I feel, despite wanting to sit there for a minute until my tailbone feels normal again, I roll to my side, grabbing the bowl with one hand, leveling the other hand on the floor, pushing myself up. The necklace I wear around my neck, always hidden from eyes, swings free. Fearful that someone will see it, I move as quickly as I can away from ma who screams at the boys now, with the boys arguing back. I set the bowl down, and quickly shove the dragon's tooth necklace down the front of my dress, out of sight again. If da were to see the tooth, he'd take it away from me. Da will return to the fire and table any minute and then the battle will really start. Da looks forward to this time of the day and now I've ruined it. Shame burns my face as I move to the fireplace to refill the bowl with food. Done, I turn and see that da is back in his seat. I serve up the food quickly but am aware that the tension is still thick, and a single wrong thing done or said can ignite a new unwelcome explosion.

Unable to stand the tension, I slip out the door before anyone notices that I'm gone. The meal isn't over, but I can't deal with it all. I need space to think and time away from these people who need me but never really see me.

From the time I learned to walk, I was always escaping to the forests. Ma says I was about three when I disappeared for an entire day. A search was conducted for a few hours, but because there was much work to be done before the dark clouds unleashed their fury on hay ready for the barns, the men deserted the search. After all, I was nothing. Just a girl child.

As dusk settled into the dark moonless night, apparently I walked out of the forest on my own—dirty, my garments torn as if ravaged, and yet, not a scratch on me. I remember da and other men, along with my mother questioning me, but how could I tell them about something I hardly understood myself? I remember when first going into the forest leaning up against a large rock. I had just rolled down a hill thick with brambles that had snagged and tore at my clothes, and the rock having stopped my fall. Thanking the rock, I wasn't surprised to hear it speak because for me, at that age and even still to this day, Nature speaks to me and always has, whether it be animals, trees, plants, or insects.

How could I tell them that a monster as large as the biggest barn in the community had kept me tucked under a wing, protecting me from a storm of other animals determined to reach me? In the scuffle with the other animals, the snapping and snarling, her chest was torn open a bit, deep enough to see muscle, and one of the dragon's many teeth had come loose. The dragon ripped it out and dropped it to the ground. Without thinking, I picked it up, pocketing it in the one special square of my dress, hidden under the apron I wore over the dress. Once we were alone, all the animals having scattered into the forest, I couldn't recall what the dragon and I talked about, but I do remember the dragon asking me not to reveal its identity—it would be our secret.

As young as I was, I already knew a great deal about secrets. I knew keeping secrets kept me from the same trouble my brothers received as I witnessed them disobey our parents and get punished. The last thing I wanted was a willow-tree switch striking me. I'd heard the boys talk about the sting that lasted well into the day after the fact. I knew, too, that to tell got us all in trouble, so I learned how to remain silent, often pretending I knew nothing while knowing a lot.

Later, when the dragon left me close enough to the edge of the forest so that I could find my way out again, I was surrounded by village elders and da, being questioned. It was easy to say I didn't remember the day, that I'd gotten lost and had fallen asleep. Much later, when I had an opportunity, I took one of ma's darning needles and found a way to string strong thread through the tooth's weakest point, weakened by decay, and wore it around my neck. No one had ever seen it, and I didn't want today to be that day of viewing. If not for the tooth, I would have forgotten my adventure of that day a long time ago.

The tooth is my talisman, the strength I hang onto.

Now, I run, determined to keep my eyes dry. I am successful, having had lots of practice. Thinking about tonight's events, I refuse to cry. I know there is no real freedom having escaped the tumultuous room. Eventually, I will have to return, to face what happened, what I did as viewed through da's eyes.

Da isn't always like this, but now that the old king is dead and his son Hrothgar has assumed the throne, rumors fly like the wheat's chaff. Da's afraid he'll lose what little land he has. Lately, I've heard him talk of an alliance.

I want to be as wise as ma, as coordinated, as fast, able to see what needs to be done without being told. Because I'm not as fast, da calls me a rebel, lazy, and worthless; yet, he doesn't see that I do the work of several women, all years older. I work steady and work just as long as everyone else, if not longer. I'm taller than many of the women, so he probably just overlooks me. Or, he's ashamed I'm not like them.

There is no changing his mind or his opinion of me, no matter what work I do, what sleep I miss, or what food I don't receive. I'm so tired. At times like this, I give up knowing I can't do enough or do the right thing.

My head down, I just walk. Decaying leaves and twigs under my feet snap and rustle, waking me from my trance. Instinctively, I sought refuge in the woods. I look up. I'm near the giant oak that is deep in the forest. I walked without thinking. Mostly, when I am this deep in the woods on sunny days, daylight is dim, with a few shadows lurking among the trees. Now, eerie black commands the night.

Strong hands grab my arms. I cry out in surprise. A large man circles in front of me. I have nowhere to run. He leans close, and I sigh in relief seeing a familiar face.

"Erik! You scared me."

He chastises me, telling me I should be scared. "Stupid girl, wandering out here alone."

Instantly, frustration gnaws at me. I have no one to blame but myself, but I don't like being chastised twice in one evening, and never by Erik. "Is there no one who speaks to me without punishment?"

"People have disappeared in these woods."

"Can't you just be happy to see me?"

He pulls me close, giving me a hug. He tells me he's happy to see me. "I can't wait to get your father's permission to marry you. I was hoping I would see you. I was coming to your house, ready to knock on the door if I had to."

I cling to his shirt, wishing I could believe him. He has yet to speak to da directly. We always meet in the forest, instead. I want us married, so that I don't have to go back home and face the consequences of not only leaving ma to clean up the mess, but for sneaking out as well. "I want to believe you," I tell him, despite my doubts.

Erik is quick to reassure me. "He'll let us, you'll see. I'm working hard to make my farm worthy of your dowry."

"Let's run away. Let's not wait for da's permission."

"You know I can't do that. I have a mother and sister to care for. There's no one else for them."

"And that's the reason why da will never hand me over to you. Your house already has too many women. According to him, a house needs men, should be full of men."

"Our children will all be boys."

"On your say-so? That's not good enough for da and you know it. You know what he's like. He has the favor of all the men in the village. He wants to be leader."

"Hrothgar will make that determination."

"But Dobson has already been appointed next leader."

"Not by Hrothgar. Besides, Dobson's as unpopular as a crow in the wheat field."

"Please, Erik, let's run away."

"We can't. Besides, you wouldn't, and you know it. You don't have the courage. Remember what happened the last time you ran away?"

Erik knows nothing about the dragon. As much as I want to tell him, I promised the dragon.

"I was a baby then. And I hadn't run away. I was lost." I fingered the giant tooth, hidden under my clothes, away from prying, coveting eyes.

"Life is hard enough without making deliberate choices you know will create disorder, not to mention banishing yourself from everyone. It would be difficult starting new somewhere else."

Erik is right and I know it, even though I don't want to admit it. Though ma can be demanding and tough, at the same time, I know her to be loving and kind when there are no men around, and I would miss our garden talks, the education in the herb garden. I still have much I can learn from her. I would miss my brothers too, both those who protect me, even though they tease me, and those who I protect and take care of. I would miss them all. I'm part of the family, part of the community. As much as I want to wander outside the community and see the world, I also know that this is home and where I belong. Maybe in time, Erik can become worthy enough in da's eyes to ask for my hand in marriage. Soon I hope.

"You're out here now because you ran away, didn't you?" he asks.

I nod. "I spilled hot food on da. An accident."

"Go back. Do the right thing. Apologize. Take the punishment. Don't let him stay angry at you. Make him proud."

"I can never make him proud. He's been ashamed of me since my birth."

"Then make me proud. You can do it. You must." Erik kisses my forehead.

I lift my face, wanting a woman's kiss. His kiss is more like a brother's than from a man I love. I tell him I love him.

"And I you," he says. Erik turns me around, so I face the house. He pushes me forward. "Go."

I sigh. I take a couple steps, then twist my head around to look over my shoulder. Erik lifts his hand and waves. He shoulders his bow and quiver of arrows. He'll be in the woods all night or until he finds food—meat for his mother and sister. I wave back at him, then face my fear, and move forward. Erik is four years older, and while I know our kisses are chaste, I know he feels the same passion and love that I do. Only twice before have our kisses become heated and sensual beyond my knowledge and experience. Both times, I wanted more. I wanted to see and experience that love that pounded in my chest and made me deaf to the surrounding sounds. Each time, however, Erik pushed himself away from me, saying it was dangerous for us to go further. How is being with the person I love dangerous? I ache to feel his arms around me, to feel his body on top of mine, to have him kiss me deeply, his hands rubbing against my skin. In time, I tell myself. In time.

Nearly at the main door of the house, I stop, take a deep breath, pull my shoulders back, straighten my spine, and wipe any and every emotion from my face. Da respects strength, not meekness, so strong I will be.

The boys are still at the table, but now they are at various tasks: arm-wrestling, sharpening a knife, or working leather. The oldest yells out that I've returned.

Immediately, da steps into the room through the second door, the one I originally escaped from. I know better than to wait for his signal. I move over to where he is, my head down in submission, my eyes cast to the floor. I stop in front of him, expecting the worst.

Quickly, I say, "I'm sorry, da. It was an accident. It'll never happen again."

"That's right. At harvest's end, you wed Angus."

I look up in horror. "No!" Instantly, I realize I said the word aloud. Surely, he wouldn't do that to me. No father can be that cruel. Angus is old, missing most of his teeth, has lost three wives already to childbirth, and has brats for children. Sickly brats and all girls, except for one frail boy. But, he has the most livestock, some of which will become da's when we marry.

"No?" Da's voice is cold, but firm. I can tell he will not reconsider his decision.

"Anyone but him, please?" I plead. I know it would be a mistake to plead for Erik, one of the poorest farmers in the village. Angus, on the other hand, is one of the wealthiest. Da covets Angus's land, but even da has to know that the land will go to the son . . . provided he lives to adulthood. Da is thinking I'll bore Angus a healthy son who lives to adulthood. The chances for a young boy to make it to adulthood in this land these days is a great plan and a huge gamble. All the villages surrounding ours are like us: large on old weak men, with gangling young boys barely into their teens. The battles with invaders extract a huge toll on our men. Da has told me often enough that none of us controls our lives, that all are at the mercy of others. How many times have I heard him say: "You have no power. No one cares about you more than we do." But, I don't believe it. He can't care for me if he's willing to give me to Angus. No, da wanting me to have Angus' son is so that da can control me and the land when Angus dies, until the son—if I have one—is grown.

"It'll be Angus or the dragon," he tells me.

I shiver in fear and take a step back. The dragon that da speaks of is monstrous, pure evil, and takes his victims easily. A mere bite, not even worthy of a meal. Not the gentle creature of my past. The screams of the people snatched in the claws of the monster, along with the stake they're tied to fill my ears. Angry that I have no power, I find myself stuttering, but do my best to subdue the anger. "I . . . I'll . . . I'll m-m-m-marry Angus."

"I knew you'd see reason."

To the boys, he announces that it's bedtime. While he hasn't spoken to me, I know it is my signal to retreat to my pallet under the stairs to the loft above, which stores hay and straw and helps insulate the house in winter. Ma and da's bed is closest to the animals—both for the warmth and to protect the critters should a stray, unwanted varmint, or thief go into the stable during the night. The boys bed down around the fire, sleeping on the bench seats that line the walls. My sleeping space is suffocating in the summer and freezing cold in the winter due to the nearby outside door and the cracks around its edges. Thankfully, the rats find no comfort near my bed, but just to make sure, when I sleep, I wrap myself thoroughly in the blanket, mending any hole when it first appears. The last thing I want or need is a rat bite.

As the house and its inhabitants settle down for the night, I listen for the familiar snores, particularly that of da's deep rattle. Soon, I know it is safe to escape. Quietly, allowing the rustle of the straw pallet to coincide with the crackles of the fire, I rise from the bed, pick up my shoes, and dart across the short distance to the door. I know just how far I can open the door before it will creak. Were I any bigger, I'd not be able to slither through the slim opening.

Erik has warned me often enough not to wander out of the house at night, but I can't stop. This is the only time when no one is telling me what to do. For the second time that night, I escape to the woods. My world is upside down and more danger filled than the forest where I automatically seek refuge.

My eyes adjust to the night. The slight sliver of the waxing moon provides enough light so I can find the deer path among the tall ferns and struggling saplings. Once the moon disappears behind the clouds, I am deep in the forest, just at the edge of a magical clearing. It is magical to me because I discovered years ago how deer like to congregate here at dusk and dawn grazing on the grasses. Tonight, the clearing is filled with fireflies and an occasional owl dips into the grass and flies off with squealing prey in its claws.

For a while, I sit with my back against a large oak, soaking up the solitude, wishing my ability to resolve my problem was as easy as sneaking out of the house.

Branches snap in the distance behind me. I listen. Deer are moving around. I can hear their soft mews. Quiet resumes.

I stand and walk to the edge of the clearing. Dandelions are everywhere here and mixed in with the grasses. I take a step forward to pluck one from the ground, when suddenly arms wrap around me and lift me off the ground.

I scream and struggle. And then I hear soft laughter.

"Erik!"

My feet touch the ground. He lets me go. I spin around, furious.

"How can you scare me like that?"

His laughter dies, and his facial expression is grim. "You deserve it. Are you never going to learn? What are you doing out here?"

"Escaping my life."

Erik doesn't say anything. His expression is funny. Serious. And something else, I can't name. Suddenly, enlightenment dawns. "You know, don't you? How?"

"Your father—"

"I don't understand—"

"I was at Angus' house earlier."

"Da saw you?"

"No neither of them did, but I heard them."

"That's where da went after dinner. But, you didn't—"

"Say anything? No. Why would I?"

"But you want to be with me!"

"I have no power. If only I were a man."

"But you are!"

"Not in his eyes."

I hate my life. I have no control whatsoever. My entire future is assumed, and I have no say. I move closer to Erik, wanting to feel his arms around me, but this time, he pushes me away.

"Don't."

I look up at him, my arms at my side. He stands there, his arms at his side, looking as awkward as I feel. Instead of looking at me, though, he stares off into the distance, over the top of my head.

"We can't. We aren't—" He looks up and sighs deeply. At least, he is struggling, too. "We have to accept reality."

"Never. Da can force me to marry Angus, but he can't force me to love him. I love you."

"Don't make it any harder than it is." Erik turns to leave.

I grab his hand. Erik pauses but doesn't turn around.

"Stay awhile," I ask him.

He turns his head and looks down at me, his face reflecting agony. "What's the point?" He shakes loose of me and walks away. Too easily. Doesn't he care?

Quickly, his steps diminish, and the sounds of the forest—the frogs, bugs, and the hoot of an owl—sound louder than ever before.

I turn around, turning my back to him. Tears threaten to spill. My heart feels as if it has been ripped out of my chest. My stomach is in knots and my mind flutters with all kinds of thoughts. I bend over and snap off a dandelion at the base of its stem, close to the ground. It's gone to seed. I raise it level to my mouth.

A twig snaps behind me the same instant I feel a breath on my neck behind me and over my shoulder. Seeds fly in the air. "Erik—"

A huge hand covers my mouth. At the same time, another hand wraps itself around my middle, lifting me completely off the ground roughly. This isn't Erik!

I try to scream but can't. I struggle to see his face.

A monster! A face like a lion. A giant of a man! I don't understand!

I kick but my efforts do little good. He carries me into a dense thicket. I kick ferociously and try to bite his hand. I struggle harder, still trying to scream. The hand covers my mouth, blocking my voice and any sound. My scream is nothing but a growl in my throat. I can hardly breathe. I'm suffocating. I try to move, but his large hand has my head locked in place. His arm is a vise around my waist. My feet kick at air. He's holding me in such a way that I can't connect to his body.

Suddenly my hands are free and my toes touch ground. I try pushing at him. Hitting him. He's solid, like a tree.

There is no escape. Whoever this is, he's far taller than Erik, wider, and far stronger. He grunts, then slams me to the ground on my back.

I have no air in my lungs. I struggle to breathe. A hand covers my mouth again, nearly all of my face, and I feel a hand under my dress.

Terror fills my soul. I scream. There is no sound, only a hoarse noise to my ears. My arms are pinned under me. I struggle to move away. My efforts are useless. His grip is tight. The forest is dark. Then, suddenly, a bit of moonlight pierces through the forest limbs. I can see enough. Pure fear grips me. An obscenely huge head, naked without hair, and horribly misshapen—larger than anything I'd ever seen before—hovers over me. His huge body smothers me. A hot, searing pain rips through me. I try to inhale but can't. My screams are broken guttural sounds caught in my throat. He growls, the sound roaring in my ear.

Tears slide into my hair. Again and again, the pain pierces through me. My body is rigid with pain. I can't breathe. I don't want to anymore. I fear this torture will never stop.

Finally, he withdraws.

The ground trembles as he moves away. I let out my breath in a sob. I inhale deeply and then gasp aloud in horrific misery. The lower part of my body is on fire. I struggle to get up. I am exhausted and weak. Finally, I am up. Every step is agony.

I don't remember walking home. I only remember seeing the house, grateful that I am nearly there.

I want to strip and wash. At the same time, I want to wrap myself tightly in a blanket and hide. I feel so dirty. Leaves and dirt cover my backside. I feel dirty inside, too. I can't risk waking anyone. Instead, I stop at the basin that still holds water from the hand washing before dinner. I lift my dress and scoop water onto my private place, hoping to sooth the pain that throbs.

I brush off my dress as best I can, then slip into the house, and into my corner. I take off my dress and slide into bed. I wonder if my dress is torn. How will I explain it being so dirty? I lay there, my arms wrapped around me, the covers up to my chin, shivering, despite the warmth of the evening. Sleep is long in coming. Despite the hot night, I shiver, determined not to cry.

I never considered myself an unhappy person, but compared to how I feel now, I know I'll never be that other girl ever again. If that was happiness, it'll be a wasted emotion on me.

* * *

I wake up exhausted. My sleep was fitful. Every noise in the night brought me to high alert, even though the sounds are familiar to me: da's snoring, the boys tossing, animals moving, rats climbing the outside walls and scampering on the thrush roof.

The dull ache in my private area is gone, though it still feels sore there. It's almost as if the event never happened. But, it had. More than anything, I fear being found out. I don't want to be found stupid and wanting, even though they will tell me I was stupid. I wasn't stupid, just not as aware as I should have been. Being in Nature is never stupid. Nature didn't harm me. Someone else did. I don't need ma or da telling me anything. I don't want to think about it anymore. I want it behind me. Just to avoid thinking about it, I get up.

I cringe having to put on the same dress, but I have no choice. I go outside and wash, splashing water aplenty so that my dress is wet. It's as best to being washed as I can perform without jumping into the river or having it off my back and being able to slap it on the rocks.

Later, when someone comments on the dirt on the back of my dress, I say that I had fallen. They laugh and mock my clumsiness. Soon they're talking and laughing about someone else.

I won't think of it.

I won't think about my upcoming marriage either.

As much as I try not to think about either, that's all I do.

My days are consumed with marriage talk that swirls around me.

My nights are consumed with nightmares—my repeating nightmare.

By day, the women around me buzz with activity as they plant gardens, planning to put food away for winter and for the wedding. My wedding. To Angus.

I escape to the herb garden as often as I can, lingering, hiding, wishing I can redo the past season. But what would have I do differently? Not go into the forest? Not meet with Erik?

* * *

As spring progresses, moving quickly to warmer weather, the days and nights blur into one another. I keep my head down, don't speak unless spoken to, do my work as expected. I don't want anyone troubling me. I am troubled enough and will explode with rage if provoked. Fortunately, everyone leaves me alone. They're ignoring me as usual or think I'm moping. I am. But, not about my upcoming marriage to Angus. I worry because my monthly menses don't come. One month passes and then a second month without a bleeding. Is it because I barely started before the attack? I know enough to worry, but I hope that maybe it is just fear, worry, and stress causing the delay. I refuse to consider the other option and I don't dare ask any questions. Plus, I'm not sick at all, so I can't be pregnant.

I know better than to think I can escape my future, my being married to Angus at mid-summer's solstice celebration, along with many other couples who marry at this special time of the year. My future is set in stone.

My heart aches with longing for Erik and extreme hurt in how he abandoned me at the first real obstacle. What would he think if he were to ever learn of that horrible evening? Would he say, I told you so? Would he care? I want him to care, to think that he could still love me.

I crawl inside myself, deep where no one can find me. My hurt is internal. I can't and won't let anyone see the pain I harbor. I trust no one. Not Erik, not da, not even ma. There is no one to turn to.

The days plod along, one after the other. I grow more tired, weary of not being able to function as I normally do. I feel depressed. I am watched continuously, so I can't escape from the house or gardens even if I want to. I am weary of conversation, especially that which focuses on the upcoming nuptials. I become numb from the heartbreak, from the pain. I can't cry anymore, even if I want to.

And then, suddenly, I start throwing up. At first, I blame the heat, the humid days of early summer, working either in the hot sun in the garden or in the stuffy, stifling house where no air moves.

Food doesn't agree with me. I have no appetite. Sometimes, just the smell of food has my stomach heaving and rolling. I've been able to hide my discomfort for a couple weeks.

As usual, the heat from the day has settled in the house and all my brothers and da are gathered around the table, clawing for their share of the food. Ma and I fill bowls as fast as they empty. Suddenly, I feel weak and have no strength in my arms or legs. I feel myself sink, my viewpoint shrinking into black.

* * *

I am on the ground, multiple voices shouting around me. Hands grab me and I'm carried to my bed. Quickly enough, by examining me, ma discovers I'm pregnant. The look in her eyes as her fingers prod me, tells me what she has discovered. How could I have not known?

Ma hisses at me, but in a whisper so no one can hear her. "What have you done? Why didn't you come to me? We could have changed everything if you had told me earlier!"

She shows no sign of compassion, no sign of caring that this is her daughter she was forced to examine. Instead, her concern is how this will make her look.

Da moves into my corner. Ma quickly removes her fingers and pulls down my dress.

"Well?" he asks.

"She's pregnant."

"What?!!"

"I was raped!"

"Liar!" da says. "You shame me. You've shamed the entire family!" To ma, he says, "If Angus finds out, he'll not want her." To me, "You did this on purpose—"

I shake my head.

"—so, you wouldn't have to marry him!"

"No," I breathe. "Not true."

"You don't want to marry him!"

"Yes, but I didn't do this. I—I—was—"

"Who's the father?"

"I don't know. I couldn't see—"

"Because you were in the woods late at night?"

"Yes."

"Seeing Erik, weren't you? Disobeying me again?"

I nod my head, looking down. There is no way I can make this right. I'm trapped. I feel like a mouse in the claws of a mighty predator. My life has no value now. I'm being forced. Forced to have a child that I do not want because it wasn't conceived out of love. Forced to marry a man I don't love. Forced to forever give up my opinions, my thoughts, my feelings. Forced to give up my voice.

I hear whispers and words that I asked for it. Why else would I be out in the forest in the middle of the night? No one will believe that I was trying to escape the brutality I suffered during the day. That day, like so many others, I wanted to get away from my family, the way they treat me, ignore me, enslave me, and brutalize me during the day. Night is the only time I can find solace and peace. In Nature.

I don't have any real friends. Someone I can confide in. Just Erik. I learned early on there are few people I could and can trust. They lie, use me, want information or knowledge they can claim as their own. I've seen others in their jealously of ma, wanting to be like ma, one of the most powerful women in the village, and how those women bid their daughters to act nice to me, hoping I'll spill a secret or two. Nor could I ever confide in ma. Early on, I learned most of what I said ended up in da's ear. And then as I grew, ma saw as a threat as I learn easily and could connect ideas where others see no connection whatsoever. Yet, she teaches me her secrets . . . or, so she tells me. I loathe her as much as she finds disgust in me. My contempt and anger is the only reason I have any fight left in me.

Now, I have betrayed everyone: ma, da, family, and community.

* * *

Da drags me to Erik's home. With no father in Erik's household, da is forced to deal with Erik directly and his mother, which I know da detests. I can tell by the way da crowds her space and towers over her, making her back up and look down in respect. I feel sorry for her. I don't understand why Erik doesn't stand up to da, helping his own mother.

I've heard da claim often enough that women have no place making decisions, that if it weren't for men, women would perish, die of starvation, that they're not much good than other for rutting and cooking the meat the men bring home. Obviously, da never tended a garden, cared for children, or kept a home. I wonder how he'd survive if he had to perform those tasks.

Without fanfare, da states that I'm pregnant with Erik's child. Erik turns bright red and looks at me horrified. Before Erik's ma can say a word, Erik sputters that wants no part of me, that if I'm pregnant, it's not by him.

Da and Erik exchange heated words before da accepts the fact that Erik never touched me. Not in that way. Erik reveals that we only kissed a few times and nothing more.

Just as da pushes me toward the door, I speak out and tell Erik, "I never claimed you were the father."

Erik just stares at me as if I'm a stranger he's never met before.

"I was raped," I add.

"So you say," da says.

"I'll not raise someone else's bastard," Erik says.

Shocked, surprised, and deeply saddened, I keep my face expressionless. The man I once thought I knew is nowhere to be seen in this man-child who stands in front of me. No wonder da doesn't see Erik as a man. The last thing I want him to think or know is that he's hurt me.

My eyes focus on the fireplace mantle just behind his head, latching on to the candle that is lit and flaming on the shelf. I can't stand to look at him directly, but I won't turn away either.

Erik has made this whole event about him. He doesn't care for me. I love him with every fiber of my being, every breath I take, so I struggle to understand how he can stand here, saying he wants nothing to do with me. So many times, I wanted to crawl into his skin, to understand him as deeply as any human can understand another.

I can't cry in front of Erik and da. I can't give Erik the satisfaction of knowing how devastated I feel right now. Nor da. I know from past experience he doesn't care.

I'll cry later. Maybe. But really, what's the use of crying? It solves nothing. It just makes me lethargic afterward, watering away my energy.

I need to let go of my dream of ever being a happy woman, to accept that I'll never be free of the shackles of my life, my sex. I'll never be free to make my own decisions. While I may think I experienced freedom in the past, I didn't, not really. I was only kidding myself. Born into a family, a village, where the price of a child is only as good as the number of chores he or she can perform without being told, without having an adult needing to direct or redo the work. Even then, the men are enslaved to the head of the village, to do his bidding. The women to men, and the children to the family.

I'll never be free. I'll never get to make my own decisions. The best thing for me now is to go along with whatever da wants, to let him believe I'm okay with my future.

The worst that can happen now is that I get sold and taken far away from this godforsaken country of mud, cold, and short growing seasons. Can it be any worse? Actually, yes. Angus. I'll be married to him and become his slave. He doesn't have to know that the baby in my belly isn't his.

I can't help but think of Erik and the life we could have had. Instead, I squash the idea down, refusing to give it life. That idea is dead forever now that Erik has rejected me. Angus is my only hope of getting away from da. With any luck, Angus' days left on this earth are few.

"I'll marry Angus," I tell da.

"'Bout time you chose the right path, though it may be too late."

Leaving Erik's house, I refuse to look back. My spine feels as stiff as my pride. My feet hurt and I'm tired. I wish we hadn't walked to Erik's but taken the horse and wagon instead, but da said the walking would be good for me. With any luck, I'll lose the baby and Angus will never know any different.

Less than an hour later, Angus declares he wants no part of me now. No part of my family either, which angers da. Somehow, someone got to Angus, gossiping about my condition. Angus claims bad luck will fall upon the family because of my behavior. He hopes that luck doesn't befall him, having initially promised himself to me.

I've never hated being female until now. Truly. Suddenly, the gripes of other women I've listened to over the years make sense. How they're used and abused and are nothing but property to be pawned off and used and abused somewhere else.

I used to believe that I could trust others even if only a little, but now I don't trust anyone. I can't believe what is said. Yet, I need others; otherwise, how will I ever survive?

I hurt so much. I can't think. I don't want to think. I stumble along the path that takes me home, da pushing me forward when my steps are too slow.

I just want to climb into bed, cover my head, and disappear . . . forever.

I'm so naïve. Trusting, loving, thinking I am loved. No, that's not true. I can't wallow in self-pity. I may have been naïve about this awful experience, but I've always known my rank, that I have little status. I might as well be invisible.

With Erik's rejection, I'm not sure I'll ever be able to love again. Trust again. I vow to never be this vulnerable in the future, but is it a vow I can make? Will I always be at the mercy of having to trust others when they've not earned my trust?

* * *

Two days later, the elders come and meet with da out in the yard. The discussion is noisy and intense, judging by the way they all flail their arms at one another, pointing and emphasizing. As quickly as the discussion starts, it ends. Da doesn't look happy as they turn and leave. He hangs his head, looking at the ground, almost as if in disagreement, in contemplation. Finally, he lifts his head, sets his shoulders, and stares at the house. I recognize that set to his mouth, his eyes steeled against having to do something he disagrees with but has no choice but to conform.

I shiver. I know I am the center of the discussion. Also, I know nothing good ever comes out of da's resigned expression. My stomach feels like it has dropped to my knees. I feel sick.

When da comes in, he doesn't look at me. He goes straight to ma, who is at the hearth, stirring the stew we'll be having for dinner. I hear her gasp, see her glance at me with fear in her eyes, and then her hands cover her face. The only time she does that is so that she can gain better control of her emotions. Usually, it takes her only a minute or less to gain control. This time, several minutes pass. By the time she removes her hands, her face is as stoic as da's.

My heart races, my skin crawls, and then I can't think anymore. My thoughts worry and tumble around with no answers, no understanding.

I'm afraid.

Together, they move as one toward me, turning me around, propelling me toward the door. Outside, we walk three abreast, they on either side of me.

They don't have to tell me where we are headed. I know. My knees feel weak. My feet stumble. I have no recourse. No future.

The decision has been made. I am merely a player in this bad story. The innocent girl sacrificed.

Am I innocent? Not in their eyes, surely. To my parents, the elders, the community, I am a threat to their security, the welfare of the whole. I deserve to die for my disobedience. All because I was not willing to be content with my station.

I have erred on the side of wanting more, a desire to be better Now, I will pay with my life.

Either the news has traveled fast or all had been decided before the elders visited our home earlier, for the entire community is gathered at the dragon stake, far enough away from it to not be endangered, but close enough to witness my body being torn limb from limb, as I am given to the dragon.

I have witnessed two such destructions—sacrifices they're called—in my young life: a stranger, who had been caught stealing pigs from an Ealdorman, and my own cousin, a young boy who refused to pick up the sword and fight our enemies. The Ealdorman and his

Council determined my cousin was more woman than man and that such disobedience could not be allowed. My aunt and uncle left the village afterward, their shame so overwhelming.

At the time, da explained that there wasn't a place in this world for weaklings or disobedience. Both sacrifices to the dragon had been earned, he said. I had disagreed but kept my opinion to myself. I had loved my gentle cousin, and I knew how he'd anguished over his more feminine qualities, his inability to kill another man. Once my cousin had said that he'd rather die than be made to kill. And so, his wish was granted.

I was probably the only one to know of his secret, realizing he was okay with his own death.

I'm not okay with mine, though. When I woke up this morning, if I had known what was about to happen, I would have left. Run away.

But go where?

Who would take in a pregnant young girl?

No one that I know of.

I shiver and feel my skin crawl. I want to throw up, but my stomach is empty having thrown up breakfast earlier.

How can I forget those images of my cousin and that stranger, with their screams of terror as sharp claws grasped and pinched their bodies, piercing into their skin and organs? Or, how the dragon bit down on each of them, tearing them in two? It is the screams though, not the blood and gore that stays with me. I feel their terror and tremble still, because of it.

After each of those sacrifices, the men in the village talked about how the two men screamed like women. To me, their screams are haunting. Worse than any animal being killed, at least those few animals I've witnessed.

I don't want to scream.

I am determined not to scream.

I become numb, my steps wooden. My parents' hands on my arms, on either side of me, propel and push me forward.

Suddenly, we are there at the base of the small incline. I look up.

The stake rises out of the ground like a dark tower, appearing large and looming from this viewpoint.

Suddenly, we are next to it. I don't remember walking up the bare incline to the post. Up close, I see the huge metal ring that hangs from the top of the post. Half my height, it probably weighs more than me.

They turn me. My backside is to the post. It is nearly the same height as me. I feel hands on me as they tie my legs together so I can't run, and then my hands in such a way that I can't untie the massive rope that secures me to the massive ring. The rope is tied around my middle with the knot in the back. A modest length of rope connects me to the ring. Were my legs not tied together, I might be able to run away from the dragon for a short time, to place the post between me and the dragon, but this way, I am an easy capture.

Facing the crowd, I look out at the townspeople who have gathered. I know that they are mesmerized, just as I had been both times I watched the sacrifice.

A huge wall of rock curves behind and around me, much like a horseshoe, partially encircling me. The hill upon where I am staked, rises nearly to the top of the rock. The dragon will perch on the rock and reach down, grabbing me in its jaws, pulling me up, stretching the rope taut until either the rope breaks or I am cut in two.

Neither thought is pleasant.

Behind the crowd is a large bell, built onto its own stand. It rings—loud and clear. Three times.

The wait begins. I watch ma, wondering why she has no tears in her eyes. I know I am just collateral to da, but doesn't she care about me at all?

And then, I hear them gasp as one. I know that gasp. They've seen the dragon in flight. He is on his way.

My knees buckle. I catch myself from going down. I straighten my spine, determined to stand tall.

My teeth chatter. I clamp down, gritting my teeth, determined they won't rattle or bang against each other. My whole body shakes. I can only hope no one notices.

I hear the flap of wings, and then a breeze envelops me.

The townspeople step back as if one, as if they are too close.

I can't stand it any longer.

I have to look.

I turn and raise my glance upward.

The dragon looks down at me, its eyes piercing my soul.

I jut my chin out and tilt my head, refusing to look away.

Suddenly, I feel no fear. And, I have no idea why.

The dragon cocks its head. Not much. But enough so that I notice. I continue staring, angry at the people. Angry I'm here. Sorry the dragon is seen as such a villain. It flaps its wings and immediately is in front of me, blocking the townspeople's view. At least, my demise will not be viewed and gossiped for weeks to come.

Whatever courage I had is gone. My time has come. Thinking I was strong, I know now that I am the weakest of the weak. I just want it to be over.

I welcome death.

No, it's a lie. I wish it true. I want to let go. Instead, I'm hanging on. Tightly. To the awful end.

The dragon bends down and I shut my eyes, not wanting to see the moment teeth clamp down on me. I hear a ghastly crunch and hear the people gasp at the same time.

Strangely though, I feel nothing. I open my eyes. The dragon bends down toward me again. I try to step back, only to stumble. Falling back, I am flat on my back because of my shackled feet and hands. The huge iron ring lies on the ground, the rope bitten in two. I am free of the post.

How can that be?

The dragon's foot grasps me, encircling me with its claws, imprisoning me tightly.

And then the dragon flies up, into the air.

I can't breathe. I'm swept away and have no control over my body. I'm dizzy, overcome with anxiety. My surroundings fade and narrow down to a small point of light. And then total darkness. I'm dying. It's the only explanation.

* * *

I feel the sun's brightness even before I open my eyes. I raise an arm to shade my eyes with my hand and open my eyelids. I sit up and look around. I'm in a small grassy clearing, though the grass is brown from a lack of rain this summer. I hear a snort behind me. Frightened, I twist around. The dragon is behind me, but lies on its belly, front feet tucked underneath. It looks as if it's been in this position for a while. It stares off into the distance, ears twitching as if listening.

"Don't eat me," I say without thinking. Why I'm talking aloud is beyond me. It can do what it wants, and I have no recourse.

"I don't eat my own kind."

I stare at it, astonished that it's responding.

"You can talk."

Suddenly, my childhood conversation with another dragon comes to mind. It wasn't my imagination back then, after all.

"Of course. So can you." It rises a little.

I notice a scar on its chest and am reminded of a battle fought on my behalf. Despite the situation, heavily balanced against me, I feel safe. Any other person would run, but I'm too curious. "What do you mean your own kind?"

"Female. The men, however, are quite tasty."

"There's no way you can be—"

"I am."

"I was three."

"Innocent and unafraid. Like now."

"How do you know?"

"I'm wise."

I open my mouth to protest. I shut it just as fast.

"Ask. There is hope for you because you know what I say is true."

I pause. "Yes."

Silence covers us, but it isn't an uncomfortable silence.

After a few minutes, I ask, "What happens to me now?"

"Whatever you want." She slides one leg out, the talons curled

She stretches her claw toward me and opens her talons. She holds my necklace with the tooth.

My hand goes to my chest, where the necklace should be. I'm surprised I didn't notice it gone.

"Your power, a reminder that you have no fear. Keep it close."

She turns her paw so that it falls to the ground, retracts her leg, and moves into a sitting position.

I rise, move toward her, and pick up the necklace, tying it around my neck again.

I look up at her and thank her. She nods her head, and then kicks a small stone toward me, one that she had been lying upon. I pick it up and notice its egg-like shape.

"You are reborn. Remember who you are."

I palm the stone. The residual heat of her body warms my hand. A strange feeling overwhelms me and then my entire body tingles with awareness.

"You are loved," she tells me.

"They gave me up. My mother was ashamed."

"Your mother knows nothing of love. All histories are dark with events that have the power to doom. Find your way."

"I have nothing. Am nothing."

"All is yours." She reaches out and with a talon gently taps the rock in my hand. "Study. You have the power."

I contemplate the stone in my hand, trying to understand its mysteries.

She stands and stretches her wings. She is huge, bigger than any hall I've ever seen. "I'm hungry." Her wings move up and then straight down. The draft is like a spring breeze, and she is up in the air.

Her shadow covers me for an instant, then moves across the land, following her as she moves quickly and quietly away from me. She moves forward into the horizon, her huge form growing small. A minute later she is gone from sight, disappearing behind the line of trees that kiss the sky.

I realize I'm hungry, too.

Earlier, fear and adrenalin overwhelmed me. Hunger was the last of my worries, then.

I'm surprised I'm still alive.

I'm more surprised that I feel at ease, especially since I have no reason to be at ease. I have no home. No idea where I will sleep tonight. No idea where I am.

Does it really matter? I'm alive.

My stomach growls. First things first. Moving toward the edge of the forest, I hope I can find some red berries on vines, maybe blueberries if I can find another clearing prolific with the ground-hugging bushes.

After walking for a while, I finally come upon a large area, just at the edge of the forest shadows, where large plump blackberries grow in clumps, with canes so heavy that the berries' weight bends the canes. I pick the berries by the handfuls. As I pluck the ripe fruit, the canes now relieved of their burden, spring back and rise in the air, almost as if welcoming the new freedom from the dragging weight.

Temporarily sated, I know I need to keep picking the berries. No doubt, they will be dinner later on, too. But how to carry them? Store them? Seeing a locust tree nearby with its large leaves, I go to it and find about a dozen green leaves, then push the stalk of one leaf into the mid-center of another, linking them until I'm able to create a small bowl. Flimsy, but solid enough. I use the remaining leaves, interweaving them, creating a second bowl to function as a liner to the first. It's a weak structure, but the weight of the berries doesn't stress the interweaving, too much. Not ideal, yet it'll do for now.

I pick more berries and fill my bowl. I hate leaving so many berries on the vine, but it would be wasteful to pick more than I can eat. Maybe I can find the bushes again tomorrow.

By the time dusk slips into night, I realize I can't remember what I've done since finding the berries. I've wandered around the forest but have found nothing. No significant streams, at least not where I can find fish. No rocks with ledges, where I can crawl under and find shade from the sun or stay dry from rainy weather.

I still don't know where I am. Having passed out when the dragon picked me up, I have no idea how long we flew. Is the village a short distance away? Or, would I never see the village ever again because we traveled so far? Will I ever know?

Does it matter?

Not really.

I think about the family, realizing they'd be inside, settled around the table. By now ma will be the only one serving the meal. She will have no help unless she is able to solicit one of the boys, but knowing da, I doubt that will happen. I want to feel sorry for her, working so hard and no longer with my help, but I realize I feel nothing.

* * *

The next few days pass in a blur. I lose track of how many days pass. The first night, I sleep on the ground and wake up in the dark, hearing loud growls close by. I climb the nearest tree and just in time. A predator that I can't see well sniffs the ground and then leaves. Obviously, it is looking for prey. Sleeping on the ground, I'm an easy target.

Since that night, I've been sleeping high in the trees. I have no choice until I can find a safe habitat.

I find just enough food to keep me going, but not enough to feel fully satisfied; but even then, these days, the slim meals aren't that dissimilar to days in the village. There were many times I'd go to bed hungry because the food didn't stretch far enough to feed me. The real difference between now and then is that no one is telling me what to do.

The next day, I happen upon some wild mushrooms, tucked under some newly dropped leaves. They are tasty at first, but then bland and not satisfying enough to ease my hunger as there are only a half dozen or so. Quickly, they are gone. The next day, I find some succulent roots and wild onions. They would be better cooked in a stew, but I can't be choosy. I brush the dirt from a root and bite down. It's bitter, but I don't care. Then, I eat one of the onions, discovering that it takes away the bitter taste of the root. I start on a second root until I can't stand the bitterness and switch to an onion. Once my initial hunger is gone, I sit and contemplate my surroundings, my life.

It's summer, and while the nights are cool, I'm not freezing. In another month, the days will become cool and the evenings cold. So far, I've been able to sleep in the trees, safe from snakes, prey, and other earth-walking dangers—chiefly man. Strangely, I haven't seen any sign of other humans. Or, is it not so strange? I don't know anymore.

I have no weapons, no tools, nothing but the clothes I wear. Up until today, this moment, I had no thought for the future.

How many hours did I spend watching the ants the other day? On a deer trail that I'd been walking upon, I saw hundreds of marching ants, some carrying dismembered parts of a grasshopper. Curious, I followed the parade and came upon their huge hill, camouflaged against a giant oak tree. Unlike my brothers who would have found a long stick to poke and prod at the nest, I chose to sit close by and just watch. Every now and then, I'd see a white egg be carried out of the nest by a worker, only to be dumped at the entrance, and then another ant would carry it off into the forest. Were these babies never to hatch, to see their mother, to become part of the colony? But why carry the dead bodies away?

Contemplating the idea, I then noticed an owl on an upper branch studying me, its head twisting sideways, its big yellow eyes piercing. Was I its first human observation? Then, suddenly, it twisted its head toward its left, cocked its head first one way, then another. Lifting its wings, it dropped from the limb and flew off, silent, and into the distance.

On another day, I simply sit on a rock for hours, soaking up the sun, feeling tired. Extremely tired. I hear fish jumping, birds chirping, frogs calling out. At one point, I turn onto my side and have a clear view of a rotting log that is half in a small pond of water, half on the dirt. The entire log is crowded and covered with turtles. They hardly move. Does the sun make them lazy and motionless? Are they as tired as I am?

* * *

Was that only yesterday? Or was it the day before? I can't remember. Nor do I care.

Despite what I think I already know about Nature, these days are filled with new experiences, new sights. Now, as I think back over the last few days, I realize my former life is already becoming a memory. I feel as if I've been in this forest forever. And yet, was it only a few days ago, I'd been removed from everything I'd known since birth?

My entire life is surreal.

What am I really doing here?

I feel lost and suddenly, vastly alone. How did I come to lie in the dirt here, surrounded by huge straight trees, pines, and skinny maples?

I don't care anymore.

I'm so tired. For the first time, I wonder what it will feel like to die. Several days ago — or is it as long as a week or two ago? — while surrounded by family, I thought I would die. But I didn't. At the time, I wanted to live. I wanted my life, my world, however bad it would turn out to be.

But this? No home, no food, hardly any water to be found. What kind of life is this? I love Nature, but does She have to be so hard? So difficult? So impossible?

I, who thought I knew so much, know little. Nothing really. Nothing at all.

As harsh as ma and da had been, this world that I have been set into is far harsher and unforgiving. Worse, She doesn't care. She just is. Something I can never be.

For the first time, I'm doubting myself. Doubting Nature. Is that what adulthood is? Knowing your limits?

Right now, my existence requires forward movement. Constantly. If not in body, then in thought. What to do next? What to eat next? Where to go? Where to sleep? To hide? To feel safe? To be safe?

I'm tired. So tired. I just can't do it. I'm hungry all the time now. I need food so I won't be tired, but I'm so tired that I don't have the energy to search for the food I need.

I want to give up. I wonder what it would be like to lie here and die. How long before my body would be scavenged by the predators? Who would find me first? The vultures or the beasts? Is it possible that nothing will find me? That I would just rot? That I could just disappear? Become enveloped into Nature's arms, fading into Her canvas?

I lie there looking up at the sky, and then suddenly I am up in the air, looking down. I'm so small! Like a worm in the dirt. And then, I move so fast upward, the trees crowd together and become small, the horizon becomes curved and distant.

A thin silver cord connects me to a ball that can only be earth, as I look back at the world from far beyond a star. And then suddenly, I am back in body, feeling the cool earth under my back.

Feeling woozy, I sit up. The movement only makes me more woozy, even dizzy. And then, the strangest sensation. Movement. In my belly. My hand is on my stomach. Is it possible? Already?

I have visions of other times, other women, other babies, the joy and cheerful chatter as babies moved inside bellies, as bellies grew. I can't feel that same joy. For me, this baby has been nothing but a burden, a loss of my freedom, but then again, what freedom do I really have?

I want to lie back down, but I can't. Suddenly, I feel protective of this small creature, this baby that will be mine.

How am I going to be able to take care of it if I can't take care of myself?

Maybe I should try to return home?

No. My family won't let that happen, no matter how sorry I say I am. Can I say I'm sorry even when I don't believe that I am? Can I live with a half-truth? A whole untruth? Wasn't I already when living there? Maybe I can find another community and find a way to ingratiate myself into their community.

As I mull over my options, I realize I have nowhere to go, that I need to stay here. Wherever here might be.

I have no clue where I am.

Will it be worth discovering where I am? Possibly, but my first priority is to find a home, to find a steady supply of meat, and worse yet, to find a way to kill those animals for the meat and furs I will need for food and warmth against the cooler weather that is sure to come. As much as I don't want to, I will have to kill to survive.

I need weapons, but I have no materials to make them, let alone know how to forge raw materials into tools and weapons.

My thinking had returned full circle. If nothing else, I need to find a community where I can steal the basic of tools and weapons: a knife, a hoe, a hatchet. I can probably make a bow and some arrows, plus I need to find some flint for fire making, but what else will I need?

I feel overwhelmed by everything that I need and don't have.

I don't have a choice. Somehow, I have to make this new life work. This is about my survival and the well-being of my baby.

For three more days, I wander around, not paying enough attention to where I am or where I've been. Nothing is accomplished, as a result. That night, as I rest once again high in a tree and safe from unknown predators, I realize I need a plan.

I'm exhausted sleeping in the elements night after night, especially when thunderstorms wake me in the middle of the night, drenching me, making the bark slippery as the rain. I don't relish having to climb another tree that night or trying to sleep in another rainstorm.

Fortunately, because of the rain last night, I am able to find enough grubs and worms easily as they come above ground, and I can eat until I am hungry no more. The rains continue throughout the day.

I know there will be no sleep tonight, not unless I actively seek a shelter.

I begin to look for rocks or some type of high landscape that will allow me to see a large area around me. And then, I realize I've been high off the ground every night. Why haven't I thought to climb higher in one of those sleeping trees up to the top so that I can have a better view of the land? Is there nothing but forest around me?

And, what about water? So far, I've been fortunate to find small streams, barely a trickle of flowing water for drinking water. Obviously, these streams can't support a solid fish population. Only a few turtles here and there. Wherever I end up, I will need a supply of fresh water.

Suddenly, it occurs to me that every village I've ever been in, which haven't been many, always had a stream close by. Why am I not seeing such a stream?

I am perplexed, confounded, at a total loss. I look up, wishing that Nature would just speak to me, help me. I am not expecting Her to do everything for me. All I need is for Her to give me a clue as to where I should go to find either shelter and food nourishing enough that I can sustain myself over the distance, rather than having to scrape the earth for only mere mouthfuls each day.

If this is to be my future as it is right now, I'll never survive. Neither will my baby. I'd rather kill us both now and be done with it before the winter winds begin to blow. I need to become like the squirrels, the bees, and the bears. Winter will limit me. Now is the time to reap Nature's bounty and harvest for when I can't fish, hunt, or search for food.

Just then, as I look up through the trees to determine the sun's position, I see a dragon fly overhead. Quickly, I turn in the direction it is headed. What do I have to lose but to follow it? Can the tooth that hangs around my neck lead me to that power I need to survive? With the same dragon having entered my life a second time, nearly a decade later, is it possible it is her again? Is it possible that for a third time, she is saving my life? I want it to be her.

I decide I have nothing to lose by following her. Walking her flight path, I find an object in the distance, on the horizon, for me to walk toward. As I start moving forward, I realize that once I reach that mark, I won't know what direction to move forward again.

Yes, I can! By noting where I had come from, I can continue, picking out new landmarks on horizons in front of me, keeping my walking line straight and true, noting the marks behind me, and lining them up with those in front of me. If the dragon made a turn in her flight, then naturally, I can no longer be following her. At least, I will be following her for a while. And, the better possibility is that I will move away from an area where I may have been walking around in circles, day after day.

I don't know how many times I reach my sighted object on the horizon and then find a new object in the distance, but I am beginning to see a different landscape. The trees are thinning a little, and up ahead, I can see a bit of a hill. Is it possible that if I climb that hill that I can see more?

Excited at the prospect, I hurry. For the first time in a long time, I feel hope rising within me. Hope is a foolish feeling to nurture especially compared to the past weeks. Ever since I took that fateful walk into the night forest, hope has been a disappointing emotion.

Suddenly, the trees disappear, and I am staring into space. I stop. The view is awe-inspiring. Water, as I have never seen it, lies before me. Blue water. I walk forward until I can walk no further. I'm at the precipice of land. Down below is a strip of barren land that butts up against this cliff.

Where am I? I sit down and try to remember all the conversations of where the men talked of hunts, of fishing, of war.

Is this the ocean or sea where ships heavy with men come from when raiding? I only know my birth village is situated next to water, running water that allows ships to dock and sail from. Nothing like this.

I notice where the coast to my left curves a little and I see water spilling over its edge. Where does that water come from? Could it possibly lead to my village? Or, will I find other villages?

I decide to investigate the water that spills into the sea. Once there, I taste it and find that it is fresh water. I drink greedily. I sigh with relief, too. At least I have a fresh source of water. Can I be as lucky and find a home nearby?

I turn my back on the ocean and head inland. Once I'm in the forest, I find a bit of an incline, a hill, and decide to climb a tree. It's the only way I can view anything from afar. From the top of the tree, I look further into the forest.

Just then, the sun breaks through the clouds. I see sun glistening on the land, filtered by trees moving in the soft breeze. These are reflections on water. From what I can tell, the stream zigzags its way through the forest and there are thin silver columns of smoke that trail skyward. Here and there are clearings with these wispy threads of white smoke being drawn up into the clouds.

Houses. I am looking at villages! The smoke is coming from chimneys. And, the villages all appear to pop up near this stream as it winds its way through the forest. Quickly, I realize I'm too close to the sea and other communities. Too close to those who arrive by ships from the sea and too close to the stream and people of these communities who travel on it. The first community looks close, though it could be an hour's hike. There is something about the village that gives me pause, as I'm able to see various buildings as the limbs sway back and forth.

And then, I see a giant pole on a hill just past the houses. It looks to be a great structure based on the height of these naked poles. Men are working around these poles, and I can see them attaching wood to these poles. Could this be the hall I had heard da talking about? Heorot's hall and Hrothgar's village? If so, my village would be further south, beyond this village. I remember da saying Hrothgar lived north of us.

How could I have lived this close to the sea and never know it?

Because I was a girl and never allowed to escape the village's confines unless I snuck out and even then I was never far from the village. Unlike my brothers who talked about seeing the sea, I was never allowed in the boats. I was too scared by the stories of Saxons and other invaders to venture too far away from home.

Shutting my eyes, I put myself back in my mother's garden, back in our house, seeing all the houses, in fact.

In that moment, a very brief moment, I am happy thinking that people are nearby, and then at the same time, the thought terrifies me. What if someone sees me? Or worse, finds me? Finds out I am alive? Where I live? Or will live eventually? What about my baby? How safe will it be from others?

I lean against the main trunk of the tree, high in the treetops, my thoughts tumbling and crashing into each other. I need a plan and it needs to be one that ensures my safety. Our safety. Will I ever be able to escape the confines of my family, community, or other people?

If I'm caught, I'll be punished again. Put to death again. I can't be caught. Ever.

I debate whether I should travel past them and try to find a home deep in the forest or stay close to the sea. If I go further into the forest, how far must I go to be safe? Is it possible I could encounter Saxons, who always invade from the south and be captured there?

I turn my head toward the right and see another reflection of water through the trees, which appears to be heading away from the sea and from this bigger river. Only this time, the reflection is thin and not as wide as this river. Can it be a smaller river, a different stream? I don't see any columns of smoke above the trees on that side of the river. I decide to investigate.

Climbing down the tree, I walk to the first river, the one that flows past the villages, and contemplate crossing it. It's moving fairly fast and I'm not that great of a swimmer. Then, I see some tree limbs traveling down the river. It's not as fast as I originally thought, but the water is moving toward the sea. One of the limbs, with several smaller limbs and its leaves, gets caught at the edge where I'm at. I grab it and decide that I can use it to help me float to the other side.

Straddling it, sitting on its thickest part, I wrap my legs around the limb, locking my ankles. I grab one of the smaller limbs and hang onto it with one hand. I push off and am quickly drifting into the river's mid-section. I start paddling with my hand and make some progress but not enough. I'll need to use both hands. I let go of the branch and lean down so that I can get both hands in the water. Focusing on the opposite shore, I paddle furiously. Soon my back hurts and I can feel myself growing tired. I rest for a minute and am swept further toward the sea, but I'm closer to the other shore than I am to the middle. I start using my feet and hands to steer me to the other side. Fairly close to the opposite side, I slip off the limb and swim the rest of the way, which ends up only being a short distance, as I find that I can soon touch the river bed with my feet. I stand and wade toward the shore. Climbing onto land, I collapse, breathing hard. I'm exhausted.

Once my breathing returns to normal, I force myself up. I need to get back into the forest. I can't risk anyone seeing me. With my proximity this close to the sea, I feel my chances of being discovered are greater than ever before.

At the edge of the forest, I find some blueberries, not quite as ripe as I would like, but I can't be choosy. I grab as many as I can, stuffing my mouth with them, as quickly as possible, and then move on. I need food to replenish my energy, but I can't expose myself for any length of time, so reluctantly, I leave the berries behind.

Deep in the forest, once again, I look for the tallest but climbable tree. At the top, I scan the horizon. I'm able to see the ocean once again. I'm not close but not that far away either. And then, I see a thin strand of reflected sun that I recognize as that second stream, slender but bright as it peeks through the leaves as they move slightly in the breeze. In the distance, I spot a width of water, wondering what it can be. Is it just a turn of the stream? Or something different? The width of reflection is too wide to be part of the stream. Maybe it's a pond of some kind.

Curious again, I will explore. The angle of the sun, now hidden behind clouds again, tells me that I only have a couple hours before the sun sets. I need to find a place to sleep.

I climb down and find some roots. They'll have to do. The landscape changes, the ground softer, almost as if the water can't drain well. The trees appear thicker and taller, with a higher number of them fallen and a large number on the ground than were on the other side of the river. I walk until it becomes unsafe because of the setting sun and find a sleeping tree to climb. Just as I am settled, rain starts falling. I wish I could find some place where I can sleep without having to climb and where I can remain dry.

The next morning, I wake hearing birds welcoming the dawn. I didn't sleep well due to the sharp cracks of lightning and the deafening roars of thunder that followed. It's early and already the air is sticky. With all the additional moisture on the ground, the day will be hot and humid. My energy will be sapped quickly, but I have no choice but to continue forward.

Before I climb down, I climb up again. As far as I can go. I want another view of the surrounding landscape. My view is hampered a bit by residual low laying fog-like clouds. I wonder if anyone from my family has ever beheld such a sight, a spectacle of various shades of green, and clearings, here and there, with small wisps of smoke arising above the trees that circle those clearings. Looking behind me, I can barely see the large body of water—the sea—anymore.

I'm making progress.

Before me, I look for clearings and thin grey streams of smoke. I see none. Good. This area appears to be uninhabited. Just the way I want it. I wonder if all the communities are on the other side of the river for some reason.

By the time my feet touch the ground, the air is saturated. Soon, my clothes are sticking to my skin, and I feel more tired than I was the day before.

I realize for the first time that I'm not experiencing sickness first thing in the morning. In fact, I wasn't sick yesterday or the day before either. Is it because I've been hungry these past few days? Or have I gone past that phase of this pregnancy?

As I travel through the forest, I wonder if any man has ventured into this area before, choosing to stay in the safer regions close to home, hunting where they wouldn't have to carry carcasses for any great distance or across that wild river? I have to believe that the baby and I will be safe as long as we keep our distance from any community and never provide a trail that can be followed.

The more I travel, the better I feel. My head feels clear and my thoughts more controlled. I need a shelter that can't be easily destroyed by wind, water, fire, or man. Or, easily seen by man. I need a home that no one can find, that no one can see, that blends well into the landscape. I need to be able to learn how to be invisible, unseen just the way my community wished.

By mid-afternoon, I stand at the body of water that I had seen from above, high in that morning tree. The water is a large pond, but it isn't spring driven, or fresh. Green algae covers most of the surface. The smell of sulfur saturates the air. Immediately, I turn away from the pond . . . to do what? I'm not sure. I stop, spin back around, and look again. The stream is nowhere nearby. So how is the water here? Surely, it has to be fed from somewhere. If it is rain filled, wouldn't it be fresher? Given all the rain of the past few days . . .

Suddenly tired, I see a rock, stumble to it, and sit. After a few minutes, I'm questioning myself. The rotten smell diminishes. Is it because I'm becoming use to it or does a breeze freshen the air? Or is that smell now part of me? If part of me, will others find me disgusting?

What others? Like I'm going to see a line of suitors trailing out of the woods?

I laugh.

Who would have me now?

I'm as far away from smelling fresh as one can get. I've lost track of how many days I've been out here, and not once have I taken time to bathe or wash any part of my body.

Looking around, I notice there aren't any birds nearby. Or squirrels. Generally, both are aplenty, scampering, and flittering among the branches. I only have a few hours before the sun will sink. Throughout the day, the temperature has only risen. For the first time, I want to take off my clothes and get cleaned up the best I can, even though I'll be climbing back into my filthy clothes.

Not wanting to hike who knows how many more miles before finding a fresher body of water, I decide I'll suffer this water. At least, it's wet. I may smell like sulfur when finished, but I'll feel better than I do right now.

Starting to strip off my clothes, I decide to keep them on. At least some of the dirt, or rather the caked mud, will melt away. Not sure of the pond's depth, I decide not to dive but to jump in feet first. I jump and gasp internally as I sink into extremely cold water. Surprisingly, under the surface, the water is fairly clear, though with a greenish tint. Still beneath the surface, I spin around and can see the dirt wall from where I jumped, plus I can see faint images of dirt walls to the right and left, but I don't see one directly in front of me. Instead, there is a white wall.

Needing air, I rise to the surface, my arms above my head, my hands splaying out to create a hole in the algae, allowing me to break the surface without wearing the algae in my hair and face. Trees surround the pond, with some trees butting up against the edge of the pond, with only a small bare beach on one side. Even then, the trees are close. Many limbs from a number of trees create a canopy for the first few feet of the mere. Could that be the reason for its coldness and for the algae?

That white fourth wall, though, has me confused. There are no rocks around the pond, so what is the white? The pond rises in an obvious circle, and then I notice. The bare beach, opposite of where I went in, is actually rock.

Curious, I dive once again, only this time, I swim directly to the white wall. Moving down the wall, I notice all of a sudden there is nothing. Once again, I surface, this time close to the bare beach. There is no way I could climb out of the water from here, so this beach is deceptive. Taking a huge gulp of air, I dive a third time, following the wall down until it stops abruptly. I swim forward, underneath the rock, which is only about two feet thick.

Quickly, the water becomes dark; strangely, so dark I can't see my hands in front of me with my arms stretched out. I take a chance and rise to the surface. If I hit rock, at least I have enough air to retrace my swim and make it back out to where I had begun.

Once again, I put my hands up above my head, so that my hands will hit any surface first. They break through the water, hitting nothing. I continue upward until my head is above water, prepared to sink quickly should there be any danger or contaminated air.

To my surprise, I find myself in a small pond of water surrounded by white-yellow rock walls. They sparkle almost as if packed with tiny shiny stars. I have no idea where I am, but I'm no longer in sunshine, and yet I can see easily enough. I can only surmise that the light-colored walls have something to do with the lack of darkness. I stay in place, not floating, not swimming, just moving my arms back and forth so that I don't sink, nor move forward.

Nothing. Just silence.

I turn around and sure enough, there is a wall behind me. I don't understand this structure. How can I be in a cave with a ceiling of rock when the ground outside was level?

The only explanation is that the water level in here is lower than the water level outside. But, it isn't. It just feels like my dive outside the wall was deeper than my ascension inside.

I spin back around, swimming forward, moving into the cave. I wait to see if anyone or anything will come out of the shadows because I've invaded their territory. Moving forward a little more, my feet touch bottom. It feels like solid rock. I take a step on it, another, and then one more until my thighs touch more rock. My hands reach a ledge in front of me. Easily, I can hoist myself up into a seating position, which then, I swing my legs over until I'm able to stand.

The air is fresh in here, not at all resembling the sulfur smell that should be coming from the pond outside. Does the stone wall obliterate the obnoxious odor?

I look up and notice that the ceiling isn't horribly high where I stand.

The cave itself doesn't appear big from where I stand but it's about the size of the house I once lived. I move to the back wall. Water trickles down the wall. I put my hands out, cupping them and catching enough water for taste. It's cold and fresh. I drink greedily.

To my left is a wall with a small hole big enough for me to climb through. Beyond appears a small room. Inside, it's cold. As cold and small as it is, it could serve as cold storage. Leaving the small room, I go back to the water trickling down the wall.

To the right is a tunnel that appears to turn to the left after a few steps. Following it for a short distance, I discover that the tunnel narrows a little, dropping down with every step and appears to make another turn. Not willing to investigate at the moment, I move back into the main room, the main entrance from the pond. How big is this cave?

Is it far bigger than I can imagine? Are there other entrances? While I want to investigate, I believe that I'll need a lighted stick to do so. To make that happen, I need grease and cloth or tar, and a stick, all of which I have none. But wait, if the walls are light-colored as they are in here, will I really need to carry a light? I take a chance that a torch won't be needed.

Looking back at this main entrance, I wonder if I could make a home here? This particular part of the cave is sizeable. I could certainly make it work. Would it be a comfortable enough home for me and my child?

My child.

What kind of cave is this? I remember hearing men in the village talk about caves, but that information came from visitors. I don't recall anyone in the village saying they'd been in a cave. Of course, I wasn't privy to all the conversations, just those that occurred in our home and, even then, mostly at the dinner table. Actually, I have no idea if anyone in the village has ever been in a cave or not.

I need to stop thinking about what I used to hear, know, or saw. But then, how would I learn about anything new I discovered if I couldn't put it into context of what I had learned in the past?

Tired of thinking, I look around.

Will I find other rooms? Will they be big or small? Suddenly, I feel suppressed, smothered, pushed down, and crushed. Is this my future?

I have to get out of here.

I turn and move to the water, to the edge of the rock floor. I sit and let myself down so that I'm standing on the ledge under water. Waist deep in water, I jump up and out. Beneath the surface, I head toward the light, back into the open. Once again, I let my hands and arms break the surface. Only when I'm breathing air, filled with sunshine, do I realize how foolish are my actions. Anything, man or animal, could have been standing there and I would have been discovered. Instantly. Could I devise a way to scan the pond's edges to ensure I am alone before ascending to the surface?

In truth, since being out in the open, living and sleeping, I've been at risk of being discovered. And it is that openness versus the all-encompassing closure of the cave just now that had me rushing out of there.

I have gotten so used to living in the open that the tight enclosure of the cave felt confining.

If I'm to live here, in the future, I will have no choice. I need to live comfortably both in the open and in the cave's confinement. I will need to be slower in rising to the surface in the future, and I'll have to peer through the surface water, scanning the banks, before emerging from the pond.

In that moment, I realize, that I've made my decision. Regardless of the claustrophobic sensation I experienced in the cave just now, it will become my home, providing I find nothing in my explorations later, as I move deeper into the cave, seeing where the tunnels lead.

The cave will be a perfect home.

First, because nothing can destroy the rock—not by any means. Nature, maybe, but certainly not from the storms the seasons bring. Not by wind, rain, sleet, or snow. Unlike straw, which can burn, and mud, which the rains destroy, there is little that can destroy this rock home, this cave. Including man.

Second, I like how it is unknown. The only way one can discover this cave is to do as I did—dive down and go under the rock into the cave. I doubt with the water this murky and algae lurking on the surface, let alone its nasty smell, that anyone will think to use the water for pleasure or drinking. One would have to be desperate in thirst or need to jump in as I had done.

Finally, I have to believe that no one has ventured this far this side of the river, with its marshy and mushy landscape, especially members from my village. No, it's their village. It's not my village anymore.

Since the village was chiefly attacked from the south by Saxons and visitors always came from the north, often traveling on the river, that means I should be reasonably safe on this side of the river and isolated from all the communities.

Actually, with all the traveling I've been doing since the dragon snatched me, I haven't seen any evidence of man until today, and there is no evidence of man here on this side of the river. Granted, I've not seen land quite like this. It is more wet than dry and not the easiest to walk on or through.

I consider further exploration of the land. But, I'm exhausted now.

How can any habitat be any more perfect than this cave? Who in their right mind would consider diving into a pool of disgusting water, expecting to find a cave?

I consider if my tiredness is sabotaging my thoughts. Maybe, maybe not.

Ultimately, before settling down into the cave, I will have to traverse deep into it, taking that tunnel path that I had seen earlier. I can't leave anything to chance. I have to ensure my safety and that of my child's.

After finding enough food to stave off my hunger, at least until morning, I return to the cave. I am too tired to climb another tree, and I'm in need of solid sleep, not one where I drift in and out, coming awake at the slightest noise or thinking that I'm falling out of a tree.

I decide to chance it and sleep in the cave despite not knowing what else resides in there. Out here, I'm exposed to the weather and the wild when sleeping in the trees. At least, I won't be exposed the same way while in the cave, particularly to the weather.

* * *

Back in the cave, I sit, waiting for my clothes to dry, which doesn't take long. Finding a small ledge on one wall, I climb up and lie down. I have no creature comforts or any bedding. But, then again, I've had nothing for the past few weeks. I'm not sure if I would like a soft bed again. For now, I don't care. I yawn deeply and find myself sinking into slumber, quickly and easily.

* * *

I don't know how long I've been asleep. I sit up, realizing I can't see a thing. Nothing. Not even my hand, in front of me. And then, I remember that I'm in the cave.

How is that possible that I can't see anything? What changed?

There is nothing but complete silence, other than the water dripping down the wall in the back.

No other sounds.

No crickets, frogs, or other usual night sounds. Is it dark outside?

In here, I can't tell.

Once again, I'm starving. The problem of being in here is that I have no concept of time. Did I sleep most of the night away or did I just take a nap?

I climb down from the ledge. I remember that the ledge is halfway between the water and the back wall. The only thing I can do is inch my way in one direction or another. Standing there, I concentrate and try to penetrate the space with my vision. Soon, I can see a vague half circle line on the floor to my left. Is this where the water merges with the cave?

I remember that the water was to my left, so I move in that direction, careful to move slowly, making sure my footing is solid. I don't want to step off the ledge and fall into the water. Nor, do I want to drop onto the rocky ledge that is in the water, breaking one of my bones. The last thing I need is a serious injury.

I feel the sensation of moving downward with each step at the same time. The incline is slight, but I detect it. It's the slope of the cave floor. While it might be easier to walk, I don't like this feeling as if I'm going to drop off the edge of the world. I wonder how long I will need to live here before I am acclimated to this space. I drop and crawl on my hands and knees instead.

The rock beneath my hands comforts me even if it is hard and scratching my palms and knees a little. It's not as smooth as I thought.

I think I'm at the pond's edge, but I'm not confident. My stomach growls loudly. I can't ignore my hunger anymore. I reach out and try to feel around. My hand touches water. I turn my legs around so I can slip my feet into the water. This routine is becoming more comfortable.

My feet feel the rocky ledge. I walk forward and the water rises up past my waist, then my breasts. I take a few breast-like strokes forward, counting them. In eight strokes, my hands hit the wall. Even though I left the cave earlier today, then I could see. Now is totally different. I need to know this cave so well that I don't have to think about it and where I am within in.

Not a lot of space between the wall in front of me and the underwater ledge I just stepped off of, but a distance I can easily remember.

Lifting my feet up in the water, I press them against the wall and push away. Once I feel I'm halfway between wall and ledge, I dive. I allow memory to guide me, but instead of trying to rationalize my thinking, I allow my instincts to take over, telling me when to stop diving and swim forward underwater, moving out from under the cave wall, and then again, up to the surface of the pond. I keep my arms straight above me so my hands will hit anything before my head does, and sure enough my hands break the surface. My head above water, I gasp for breath but realize I'm not truly winded. Fear had me gasping. I've got to trust my instincts more and push fear down and out of my thoughts.

No wonder I couldn't see anything in the cave. It's darker than I've ever seen it out here. No moon, no light. Apparently, what light is in the cave occurs due to the sun's reflection in the water.

If I am going to survive in this wilderness of Nature, I need to work with Her, not against Her. I need to overcome all my fears and truly rely on Nature and my instincts. Of course, there is much still to be learned if I'm to survive and when I think about Nature and all that is here for me, I feel comforted for some reason. I need to test my instincts so that I'll know beyond a doubt when they're speaking, talking to me.

As I swim to shore, I become fully aware of the night, the sounds, the normalcy that tells me all is well. Climbing out of the water, I welcome the hot evening air, high in humidity that clings to me like a second skin.

Night gloves the landscape with a thick veil of mystery and mysticism. Fireflies float above the grasses and in between trees. Looking back at the pond, I notice that it disappears into the night. I can't detect where the land ends and the water begins.

I wonder if I were to light a fire in the cave if that light would get reflected out into the mere and could be seen from anyone standing at the mere's edge, where I sit now. The only way to answer that question would be to light a fire in the cave, and then swim out and observe.

Just thinking about the logistics of fire making makes me tired all over again, but I already know I will be spending a good portion of my time during non-winter seasons gathering food or killing for food, and gathering wood for hibernating purpose during most of winter. Actually, the only difference between now and my previous life is that I will be doing all the work, minor and major. All of it. I'm saddened that I have no garden to tend, but then again, won't I need a garden of some kind? I will, I decide, but I'll have to create one that appears part of the natural landscape. No straight rows out here, otherwise, I will be found. Guaranteed.

My stomach growls again, reminding me I can't sit here like this any longer. There is something about this place that makes me reluctant to move, however. I enjoy listening to the frogs, whose calls sound louder. Even the air is clearer. Is it possible that it rained while I was asleep and in the cave? Possibly. I'll no longer hear the wind or rain when in the cave, I realize, not unless it's a major storm.

I think about my past fear of storms, how the roof of the house felt as if it would collapse any minute with each bolt of thunder. I laugh. No worry about my roof falling in now. Not here, not anymore.

The more I think about the cave, the better I like the idea. I won't need to create a shelter from scratch or worry about fire. Building a fire, yes, I need to create. I worry about how I can gather the wood. At least a fire will never destroy my home. Is it possible that a fire in the cave will be warmer than a fire in a mud, stick, or straw house? Only time will tell. Gathering wood will be a full-time activity. Not only in the gathering, but in swimming it into the cave, and then drying it out before I can use it. Too bad there isn't another entry, but then if there was, the cave would be less of a fortress than it is already.

I spend the evening foraging for food. While more difficult at first to navigate the forest in the dark, after a short time, my eyes adjust, and I become more adept at feeling and sensing what is around me. I hear bugs crawling. I feel the slight movement of air as an owl flies nearby. I become attune to the air itself and can feel the vibrations of others—creatures of the night—as they move around. Once again, I'm becoming one with Nature. I relish the sensation and welcome it, much like a reunion with myself.

Dawn finds me back at the pond, my hunger gone, and with a greater satisfaction than I have felt in a long time. I dive into the pond, knowing the way. Quickly, I'm in the cave. Still feeling euphoric about the evening, I decide now is the time to explore the cave. I move to the back wall and stop. I have no fire, no light.

I don't want to wait.

I'm ready to check this cave out fully now. I don't want to invest any time into making it my home, only to discover that I didn't check out any hidden dangers or possible discovery from others.

Going to the back wall, I turn and move into the right tunnel. After a few twists and turns, the path takes a sharp turn to the left, and in front of me is a hall with walls and a ceiling that twinkle with hundreds of iridescent lights. I've seen rocks like this but never entire walls of rock.

I follow the tunnel and move through another doorway that opens into a room that I can only describe as magnificent. The ceiling is high, higher than most trees. The length and width is immense, and a waterfall, though slight, spills on the wall opposite me. I wonder if this water is somehow the source of my pond as water spills into a seemingly hole in the ground and then the water disappears from view.

Suddenly, to the left of the waterfall, a huge rock moves.

Dragon!

And then, I recognize the scar on its chest. My dragon.

"How did you find me?" she asks.

"I didn't. I mean, I did but it wasn't my intent. I just . . . I mean, I wasn't searching. Just exploring. The cave on the mere. I'm looking for a place to live, where I'll be safe . . ." I pat my stomach. "For me and my child."

"Child? So that's why—"

"Sacrificed at the stake? Yes."

She doesn't say anything.

"I've intruded," I finally say. "I'll leave."

"No. You'll stay. No one would suspect I would live with a mere human."

"Thank you." I turn to leave.

"Wait. You need fire." The dragon breathes fire on a small length of wood. "Take it and any other wood you find in here. I don't need it."

I move to pick up the few sticks of wood I can see, and then move toward the stick that now burns at one end.

"Come see me again in two days' time."

With that, she flies straight up, and then, with her wings pulled in tight against her body, she disappears from view. I can only imagine that she is flying through an opening that I can't see.

I spend the next two days doing nothing but hauling rocks and wood from the forest and foraging for food. My fire is a hungry animal, licking greedily at the wood until the flames find an opening into the wood's core, making it scream with hissing cracks and groans, sending streams of white smoke up toward the cave's ceiling, which then changes into a veil, draping, and spreading across the ceiling. Initially, while I thought the cave would become cloudy with smoke, creating a thick, fire-like smell, replicating that of the lodge where I had lived, instead the smoke remains only on the ceiling, slowing drifting and dissipating as it reaches the apogee of my cave and escapes down the long tunnel, but when I go into the tunnel, there is no smoke. Where does it go?

I go outside and look around, but I see no smoke coming out of the ground anywhere. I'm puzzled. If I can't see it inside or out, will anyone else be able to see it either? Should I worry about it?

In the end, I give up. I decide that if I can't see it, no one else can.

That first day, I have a roaring fire going but quickly find that a smaller fire does just fine. That night, as I return to the cave after a foraging for food, I can see the pond has a red glow to it and has an appearance of being on fire itself. The fire inside has to be the cause. While I've noticed the smaller trees, for the first time, I notice that the pond is surrounded by several large, gnarled ash trees, with several branches hanging over the water. Obviously, some of the debris in the mere is tree born.

Indeed, once I'm inside the cave, the entire room is aglow. I need to consider if this new characteristic will be a good thing or bad, especially if someone were to happen upon the pond. Will the red glow intrigue them or scare them? I decide it would be the latter considering the tales, the stories I used to hear men talk about.

On the second day, coals line the fire circle I created on the side of the cave where I plan on sleeping. The rocks I hauled in here create a border to contain the fire. I'm glad I made the effort. The coals are the keeper of the flame, and they will provide enough heat for both cooking and warmth. It will be interesting to see how much of a fire will be needed for winter. Since the cave isn't open to the elements, I have to believe that regardless of the weather outside that the cave's temperature will prove constant and reliable.

With even a small fire, I'm provided enough light to see all the cracks and crannies in the rock. As I stare at the rock, I notice the crystal details and other elements in the rock. While the crystals are not as plentiful as in the big hall leading to the dragon's cave, there are crystals enough to generate an interesting glow, an almost ethereal setting. Like having stars in the sky, but here, they are stars that shine day and night, all without a tree line to obstruct my view. My own dynamic, yet contained skyline.

I already know that the floor is not wholly level. But how bad? I go to the pond, cupping my hands, dipping them into the water. Quickly, I walk part way across the floor and open my hands, dropping the water to the floor. Fascinated, I see the water bead up, small beads joining others, until it's all running back to the pond like a small river. I'm okay with the imperfection because the cave floor is smooth enough despite its slant; in fact, I doubt I'll have to sweep this floor at all. Actually, any liquids that end up on the floor will drain into the pool, which will be a good thing, especially when gutting and cleaning any animals.

Because of the floor's smooth incline, I wonder if water used to stream through here from the dragon's lair before returning to the pond. I strongly suspect the water from the dragon's waterfall ends up in my pond somehow, which explains both its cold temperature and clarity beneath the surface. While there is stagnation and smell on the surface, that doesn't appear to be the case throughout the body of the water in front of me, here in the cave. I continue to ponder about the water's clarity, wondering if it will always be this clear. If it were to become murky, all the better so that it could hinder someone else finding out about the cave, my hideaway, my home. My fresh water comes from the waterfall on the back wall.

I end up spending much of the day exploring the various nuances of my enclosed environment. Intimacy of this environment cannot be a stranger. I need to know my habitat's feel, its smells, its sounds. I need to know its walls, its space, its safety, and its dangers. I need to know it as well—if not better—than I know myself and Nature outside of this cave and in the woods.

While I couldn't find any smoke coming out of the land above me right now, that doesn't mean I'm fully safe. I'll have to check the smoke's emission through different seasons, different weather, just to make sure.

* * *

Finally, the two days pass, and I'm able to meet with the dragon.

As soon as I enter her chamber, I notice that there is a pile of wood dumped in a heap, complete with smaller branches still with leaves and needles, depending on if evergreen or deciduous.

Our meeting is short and the expectations equally short. Basically, I am to do nothing that will endanger her, and she will do likewise; the goal is to keep our whereabouts secret from the world. I'm in total agreement.

She is honest enough to say that she considers me her alarm to intruders coming in from the pond, which is the only way in. There is a secondary entry, but she tells me it's a deep hole in the ground with crumbling side walls. She doubts anyone would venture down it, simply because there are no footholds in the walls. It's a long drop down . . . straight down. Anyone trying to descend the walls would fall to their death.

What she is willing to do for me in exchange for my being her alarm is to supply me with wood. I am surprised and grateful for this gesture. Her generosity will allow me to spend my time hunting and getting ready for winter. She will leave wood at the entrance of her chamber, which in the future will block the entrance, but other than that, she prefers that I not disturb her. She claims that she's been a solitary creature for several hundred years and she's not about to change her ways now. I respect her wishes and understand how she feels. Her only other request is that I don't bring any animals into the caves—live ones that is. No pets, livestock of any kind, or anything she would find tempting to eat and cause me sorrow if I were to befriend such animals. In fact, she states that the best animal is a dead one. Including man.

Frankly, I can't disagree with her.

I ask her how she'll feel about my child when it's born. She admits that she's not ecstatic about the idea, but because she rescued me, it'll be her cross to bear. Hopefully, it won't be rowdy or loud. I promise her to do my best.

With my fire already lit, for a few hours that night, I carry wood, dragging the larger pieces, into my chamber. I lose track of the many trips I make, until finally, I am so exhausted I cannot carry one more twig.

Now I set about stripping the leaves and needles from the wood, placing the soft material on my sleeping ledge. Soon I have a sizeable layer, enough to cushion my body and head from the unforgiving hard rock surface. I snap long twigs into smaller bonfire-size pieces and stack it nearby. The twigs I can't snap and the longer, thicker branches that are the width of my arm and bigger, I leave for the time being. I have no tools at hand.

Mentally, I list various tools that I need, along with other supplies, like a blanket or two, sewing needles, an axe, a knife or two, and even a pot or two so that I can cook. Somehow, I will need to accumulate these goods and more that I haven't thought of if I'm going to survive.

Weary, I put a couple sizeable logs on the fire and then stir the coals, covering the logs so that the coals will cook the logs without a lot of air to create high flames.

Satisfied, I lie down and instantly am yawning, feeling my eyelids drooping.

* * *

My skills as a hunter are pathetic in the beginning. While I may have thought I had enough skills needed to take care of myself, actually performing these skills is entirely different. It takes a week before I catch my first rabbit. At first, I try simple lures, such as using a vine as a rope, but I am never quick enough and dislike having to lie in wait, sometimes for hours. Such a waste of my time.

Then, I try crafting a basket-like trap, created with vines. With one side held up with a stick, my attempts are again futile because I'm slow to respond. The rabbits have better reflexes than I do. Plus, I still need to remain with the trap to spring it. Finally, I find a huge pile of brush, formed when several trees had come down close to each other in a storm not too long ago and where a number of rabbits are burrowed deep within. I can tell by the fresh tracks outside the pile that this is home.

After a day of watching them come and go, I choose one of their many paths, but one less frequently used and dig a hole in the middle of the path. The digging is slow with only a flat rock and a stick to work with, but once I get a few inches down, the soil is soft and easy to remove. Then, with extremely thin branches, I cover up the hole, hoping the rabbits—at least one rabbit—will fall in, but without taking any branches into the hole with them, which they can then use to climb out. The first attempt is a failure. Apparently, I didn't dig deep enough as there are hare footprints in the hole, with one side dug out a bit. I make the hole deeper.

When I come back the next day, I see that I have my first catch. I kill it by striking its head with a rock. I struggle gutting it and removing the hide, as I don't have a knife but only sharp rocks, which are too dull for this kind of work, but that night I have fresh roasted meat for the first time since my dismissal from all society.

Unable to use the fur for much of anything since I did such a poor job of skinning it, I add the bits of fur to the top of my bedding. Eventually, I want to have a bed full of furs. They'll be handy come winter.

I can't avoid the obvious any longer: I need better tools. Knowing I'm not able to make them myself, nor not having the time to do so even if I had the skills, I realize I have no choice. I need to steal what I can, what I need from the village. My old village.

Now that I've made the decision, I consider what to retrieve. As my list gets long, I realize that I'll need to make two trips, if not three. That's unfortunate because it puts me more at risk than I'd like. I can't do it. I need to make one trip, taking only the barest of essentials.

Because it is late in the season for me to start my own garden from scratch, I decide to take starter plants from ma's garden. She owes me. For all the abuse, for not supporting me, for not saying anything at my sacrifice. For not loving me.

It's not like she'll miss anything, what little I'll take.

But where to put a garden? It needs to be a wild garden or have the appearance of one. It can't look tended. Its creation has to appear natural.

I remember an area in the woods that had fewer trees and wasn't as marshy with lots of rocks. In fact, there was a circle of larger rocks, all surrounded by marsh and isolated. I doubt whether anyone would purposefully travel to that area because it was so far within the marsh. I could easily plant there. It wouldn't be a fun journey there to harvest, but it would be safe.

I happened upon this area, this pile of circled rocks within the forest the day I was tracking a lone she-wolf. I saw her, with milk-filled teats, acting skittish, constantly looking behind her. It is rare to see a wolf alone. Curious about her and her den, I spent the better part of a day following her, tracking her prints, which included her moving into the marsh. Generally, animals skirt around wet areas, but this wolf had a secret stash of pups she apparently didn't want found.

At one point, I stopped and listened. There were no birds flying around, and the forest was still all of a sudden. I looked around. I could sense danger but couldn't see it. I tensed, prepared to move quickly in any direction. The only weapon I had at the time was a spear, a strong thin, long length of straight wood where I had made one end pointed by rubbing it tirelessly for two days against stone.

I heard growls, but not the soft calling growls of mates or mothers to young. These were danger-filled growls. I climbed the nearest tree. And just in time. Two bears. And, the female wolf I was following. They were hassling her, and she was backtracking to keep her pups from becoming their next meal. I watched as she led them back the way both she and I had traveled. Generally, bears are solitary creatures, so I had wondered why they were teamed up. Watching them, I saw that while large, they were still young. I decided they must be siblings deserted by their mother but not having separated from each other, yet. Had they been full-grown bears with more experience, they would have killed the she-wolf already. I wondered if she knew she was playing with adolescents. I think she did but because there were two of them, she was outflanked.

I couldn't stand it any longer, seeing her becoming exhausted. I yelled at the bears, only my yell sounded more like a growl. The bears immediately took off running. The wolf, though, more experienced, crouched down, not moving. She sniffed the air, trying to find this new enemy.

"It's okay," I said.

She startled, then looked up, spotting me. She stared.

"I'm not going to hurt you." She was still in a defensive stance, ready to escape, but her ears weren't flat as they had been before.

I would never kill a mother, never knowingly. Especially one with youngsters. I will if it means my life or hers, but not for food or fur.

She sat up and cocked her head. I said a few more reassuring words. Deciding I'm not a danger, she looked back where the bears had taken off, then headed off in the opposite direction, the one she had been taking originally. I waited until she was out of sight before climbing down. I wanted her to feel safe. I had no desire to kill her or the pups. I just wanted to see where she was headed, especially if we will be sharing the same area.

I continued to follow. That's how I happened to come upon this small semi-clearing and an even smaller area that was mostly surrounded by large rocks.

The moment I saw the area, I knew it would be good for a secret garden, putting plants in there, making it look as if they had grown naturally. At the time, I decided I'd put some plants in the rock cracks and other awkward spaces to make it all look more natural. At the time, though, I had no thought of where those plants would come from.

Now, I do.

My plan is to get some shoots, preferably, as they'll have roots rather than taking cuttings that I'd have to root myself. To take any part of a main plant means possible discovery. Shoots won't be missed.

Then I have to replant it all and hope that they do well in this shortened growing time I'm provided. Ma used to give shoots of plants to women from other communities. She would say when handing off the plants, that it would make her garden all the stronger. "To give is to grow." Ironic as I think about that saying now. She could give to everyone but me, it seemed. I decide to help her garden grow a bit more this year. She'll be giving to me as she never did in our relationship. Besides, if she really believes in that adage, she doesn't have to have knowledge of her giving.

The best time to get the shoots would be either in rainy weather or bad weather, when most of the village members would be inside, huddled around their fires. Truthfully, it would be better to transport the plants in rainy weather than on a hot sunny day where the plants could dry out more quickly.

I decide that I'll take small healthy plants, just pulling them from the ground not caring if they'll be missed or not. If I'm not greedy with the bigger plants, maybe she'll believe some wild animal attacked her garden. In a way, she wouldn't be wrong. I am a wild woman now.

But, what if there is someone outside? I can't afford to be seen. I have to disappear, to be able to disappear. I had seen the village prophet disappear and then reappear right before my eyes once, though she didn't know that I was watching. Or did she?

Da used to laugh, saying no one could disappear completely, but I noticed that ma never agreed with him. She never said she disagreed, either. She just never said anything. Her silence made me wonder if she knew more than she was saying.

That one and only time I saw the seer disappear, she hadn't used any tools or plants. One minute she had been walking toward me where I was hidden in some bushes. And then, suddenly, she wasn't there. And yet, I could hear her moving past me, the leaves underfoot crackling and crumbling. I saw a foot impression appear, as by magick, on the path's dark soil. So how had she done it? Was it possible that through her thoughts alone, she was able to become invisible?

Could I make myself invisible?

While I wait for the weather to turn and drive villagers inside, I practice. Having been so pre-occupied these past few days, I've not had an opportunity to just sit and enjoy Nature. I think back on the serenity and happiness I experienced when in the woods in that earlier so-called carefree time. I need to return to that mindset, to become one with that Nature again. As I consider Nature, I realize back then that I'd only known Her surface, not realizing that She would be deeper than any well or hole in the ground.

For the next couple days, after I've retrieved enough wood, have found enough food to fill my belly, plus put some in reserve, I go into the forest. At first, I just sit and listen to the sounds. Then, I sink into the sensation of being. I recognize that here, there is no worry, no thought of future other than preparation, the gathering of food for bees, ants, squirrels, and other animals. Some birds hide nuts in the trees, creating a cavity with their bills, but many other just eat. I notice how all the animals stay out of each other's way unless there is intent to trap, catch, and devour.

And then, I hear a new sound. Whispers. Chatter. And yet, there is no one else around. Suddenly, I realize I'm hearing the trees, talking to each other. These are families: siblings, parents and children, grandparents, and even great grandparents. I hear the groans as they rub against each other, cracks when a twig is broken by a scampering squirrel or a too-big bird of prey attempting to perch. Soon, I hear words of wisdom coming from these numerous trees and plants: live well in Nature, give what you can, take what you truly need but no more. Just be.

I'd always been drawn to the flowers, but now I study all the plants. I lie on the ground and study the plant stems, noting which are smooth and which have hairs, and watch as new leaves unfurl slowly and open themselves to the sun. I watch ivy climb the trees, imbedding new roots into the bark as they grip their way upward.

I watch a colony of ants march en masse across an expanse of dirt and faded leaves from last year's fall and attack another colony of ants. The first colony races into the nest of the second colony and reappears with their booty: the bodies of full-grown ants or larvae. Quickly, they scurry back to their own colony. I look up and see an eagle, with a rodent in its jaw, fly to a branch and just sit there looking around. Then, I spot a large nest nearby. Sure enough, the eagle flies to the nest and drops the meal. I'm not able to see any birds in the nest due to its size. Immediately, the parent flies off. Minutes later, another eagle, this one much bigger and with slightly different markings, lands on that same branch the first eagle had used. Again, this one looks around, but this one has a rabbit in its clutches. I watch for some time as these two birds of prey, parents obviously, take turns bringing live food—moles, squirrels, rabbits, birds, rodents, and fish now and then—to the nest.

At the edge of a small meadow, one where I know deer cross from one thicket of trees for another on the opposite side of the meadow, I wonder if they will pass with me in close proximity. I decide to test my idea of invisibility. Ideally, if I can become invisible, I will have a safer time of sneaking into the village to retrieve what I need to survive well.

I find the heavily used deer trail that winds into the meadow. The path is narrow but well-trodden. I find a spot in the middle of the meadow, next to the path, where I am fully visible to the deer regardless of which direction they appear. I sit about three feet from their path. The sun is fast disappearing behind the trees, and in another hour, it will be dusk, the golden time for deer to move. I have that hour to meditate and get my mind clear, so that I can focus on my disappearance.

I cross my legs and straighten my spine so that I am sitting straight, without slouching or bending. It's a comfortable position. I have no idea how long I have been sitting like this, when suddenly, the world, my surroundings fade away. Rather than hearing the sound of many crickets, I hear only one. Loud and distinct. I feel the slight shift in the air that occurs from the overhead flight of a bird or two. And, then, I hear them. A snort. A bleat from one animal to another. I hear the rustle of grasses as their bodies brush up against the tall, green, willowy reeds. Then, I hear footsteps. Soft. Deliberate. Steady, yet cautious. And then, they are here, just a few feet in front of me. A few appear to look at me and yet appear not see me. It's as if they are looking through me and at something further away in the distance. The same few stomp their feet, ears alert and, indeed, are looking through me and beyond. From behind me, I hear a growl. I want to turn around to look but don't dare. And yet . . .

Suddenly, the deer take flight, tails up, and they scatter quickly into the woods. A lone wolf brushes past me, so close that I can smell his fur and hear his panting as he gives chase.

Startled, I gasp slightly, quietly, careful not to make a sound. Suddenly, there are more wolves, streaking past me, on either side of me. Surely, as a pack, if they are seeing me, they would have attacked. I've seen them attack grown men before. How could they not see me? Unless—

Is it possible that they didn't see me?

I sit there stunned at the possibility. Did I really do it? Even now, I wonder if I'm still invisible or in my consideration of the event, I made myself visible.

I listen. I hear only the sounds of the wind, birds, and other sounds that signal safety. I hear no hoofs running, no growls, no heavy breathing of a panting animal.

I get up and return to the cave. All the way, I ponder over this event.

Over the next few days, I make myself vulnerable, testing my ability to disappear into the wilderness in full view of various animals. Only when I purposefully bring myself out of my invisible mode, do they see me and take flight, whether by wing or hoof.

My next test is to remain after I return to visibility, and then move minutes later. If I move right away, I can't prove that the animals' flight isn't due to my becoming visible. Test after test, time after time, only after I shift into visibility without any movement on my part, do I see the animals look at me, truly seeing me for the first time. A few startle and are on guard, ready to take flight if necessary. Only when I move, do they move as well.

I become confident and more connected to Nature than ever before. It's as if I've been given magick powers where I can hear, sense, and feel beyond human capabilities. Is it because I listen? Or was I so busy with the mundane, filling my life with noise that I was deaf to the magick at my fingertips, in my entire being? It's as if my senses have risen to a new level. I'm more keenly aware of my surroundings, that which I can see and hear, and that which I can only sense. I'm beginning to trust what I sense more than what sounds rational or practical.

With each test, once I've become visible again, I get up slowly, doing what I can, not to appear as a threat. Over time, most animals, especially those living in close proximity to the mere and cave, become use to my movements and we ignore each other with respect. Consequently, I hunt outside of this new protected area. Let animals elsewhere be wary. Here, near my mere, I need the help of the animals, their assistance as watch guards.

I learn to trust their chatter. If there ever were to be no noise when I emerge from the mere, that's when I will know I am in danger, that someone—or something is there wanting to harm me.

Unfortunately, as much as I trust animals over man, the only way I will ever be able to determine if I can indeed become invisible is to involve man.

Can I afford to take that risk?

Do I have a choice?

If I'm to gather tools and plants from the village, from my mother's garden, I have to take that chance.

Finally, the perfect day arrives, a rainy, cool day that will drive village residents inside. With some deer hoofs that I take from a much-decayed carcass I found in the woods on one of my ventures, I begin hiking toward what I anticipate is the direction of the village. As I walk for what feels like half a day, I begin to chastise myself, believing I should have sighted some markers along the way. I start paying better attention to where I am going and where I've been. I want to know these woods as well as, if not better, than the woods I used to haunt by day and night. But then, I remember, I'm on the other side of the river. I don't know these particular woods well.

I continue to head to the village, to the other side of the river. I need to find a place where I can cross without leaving a trail or being observed, and I need to stay in the forest rather than walking the banks of the river. Because I need to observe where I am without being seen, to ensure that I blend into the landscape, I smear dirt and mud on any exposed skin, plus I carry a big enough branch that I'm nearly invisible should anyone be looking across the river in my direction. I walk several yards within the forest, staying in the shadows, just to be sure.

I've been walking too long. Is it possible that what looked like a short distance from atop the tree that I miscalculated? With every step, I become more worried, wondering if I had, indeed, gone past the village, when finally, I see smoke above the treetops.

Soon, the village is in sight. Because there was nowhere safe to cross the river before coming upon the village, I have no choice but to pass it. My old world. I travel another half hour or so before I spot my opportunity to cross the river without having to swim it. A major tree has fallen in the river, almost connecting both banks. It looks like a newly fallen tree, too, from a recent storm no doubt. Lucky for me, it's fallen where the river is narrow, nearly connecting the two sides. I can use it as a bridge, easily enough.

A few minutes later, I'm standing at the roots that are totally exposed to me, and which are far taller than me. The tree is far bigger than I wanted. I have to wade out into the river a short distance before I can climb aboard the lowest branch, which is in the water.

Balancing myself, my steps become secure as my toes grip the wood, and I'm quickly on the other side. I don't see any tracks on either side of the river, so no one has discovered the fallen tree yet. I wonder if anyone is traveling the river from further south and can get to open ocean. It's hard to tell. My knowledge of this river is so limited. I don't like not knowing. I make a note to be more observant. I need to start watching and studying the river as I do the animals and plants.

A short distance from shore is a mud wallow. I see prints and body prints from animals who have used it. I use it, too, smearing new mud on every surface of my skin. I roll around in the mud like a happy pig. I used to wonder why animals liked having mud on them. Now I know. Living out in the wilderness as I do, the mud eliminates most of the mosquitos and fly bites I would receive otherwise. Additionally, the mud lets me blend into the landscape. No longer do I think about getting clean or staying clean. Instead, nearly every day, I muddy up, both to mask my whereabouts and to keep my scent from hungry mosquitoes. Smelling like the animals helps when tracking or trying to hunt, too. Thinking about hunting, I'm happy that after tonight, I'll have the appropriate tools to kill, cut, and skin.

Back in the forest, but now on the village side of the river, the worst thing that could happen does. The rain stops and the sun comes out. Immediately, I feel the difference in air temperature as the sun begins warming the ground. A mist starts rising. Humidity becomes thick, which means that the villagers will be coming out of their huts, enjoying the sun, and continuing with chores they started earlier before the rain.

My only choice is to hunker down where I can watch the village from a distance or return to the cave. Hoping that the weather will change again in my favor, I decide to risk waiting out the weather rather than retreating for another day. I'm running out of time. I need to be at the ready and strike quickly.

I need a place to hide. But where? I need to be a good distance away from the village, but where I can still watch it from the south, which is the back of the village, where my family's hut stands.

Looking at the area with fresh eyes and a new purpose for familiar territory, I find a craggy rock face, dragonhead high and twice as long that offers protection for me from the occasional wind that pre-tells of the cold to come. Though today, it's a swirling sweltering heat and hard to detect any wind's origin. This spot will work well because it's up on a slight hill, too.

The rock face is bordered by a row of greenery that hides me from sentry eyes. I'm able to hide between the thin space between rock and green, just enough for me to stand unseen or even lie if needed. It doesn't take long for the rocks to warm and reflect the heat, creating a womb-like atmosphere. I know no one comes this way, particularly because of all the thistle and nettles that dominate the area between here and the garden. While I've never been in this one spot before I'm able to avoid the pricks of the plants. My earlier mud bath insulates me easily.

I settle down, knowing my first opportunity to raid the garden and much needed supplies won't occur until nightfall. As I watch and wait, I realize that they may have exterminated me from their community, but they are not rid of me.

As night descends, I'm sheltered in the very confines of what frightens the villagers the most: the dark unknown. What they think they fear are those like me: creatures who inhabit the dark. Yet, what they should fear most are themselves, the monsters within, monsters of their own making, for I was one of them. Now I am the creation of their mind, magnified by their fear.

I am like them with desire, wants, company, comfort, and the need for love. Unlike them, I am hungry, so hungry. That hunger makes me more dangerous. I smell their fires. In my mind's eye, I can see the fires blazing in the middle of their homes, a pit located in the center of the house or in the wall. I can see the tripods and hooks holding pots and kettles, with soups and stews boiling, children huddled around the fires' edge for light and warmth, meats sizzling, fat dripping into the hot coals, hissing as the fat sizzles away, leaving a greasy residue.

Fires outside the structures are meant to scare the creatures of the forest, but I'm not scared. I'm amused. Fire doesn't keep me away. Fire doesn't keep other creatures away either. Fire lets us know that food is nearby because only humans use fire. Animals eat their food raw, which is how I eat most of my food these days. After that first rabbit I cooked, the next one I couldn't wait to cook as I was so hungry. I never cook the bugs or worms I eat. Any fire I have is for heat and boiling water. I can't seem to tolerate the stench of cooking meat anymore. Maybe that preference will change after the baby is born.

I don't know the particulars, but I've learned that if I don't boil water, I become sick with loose stools. Only drinking water that has been boiled am I able to avoid this sickness. Is it because the waters are fouled somehow? While the water looks clear enough when I capture it from the wall inside the cave, and I was okay with it for a short time, does the mere itself influence the waters nearby? Especially if drinking large quantities of it?

As much as I've puzzled over the water's ability to create sickness or keep me well, I'm not able to create a definitive answer.

Beyond the fires, beyond the homes, up on a distant hill toward the sea, the skeleton of a structure looms in the moonlight and the fires lit there. Hrothgar's hall. I never could see it before. But then, I'd never had this vantage point before, either. There had been talk of the building when Hrothgar became king and when he made that location his. I remember that talk from last winter—was it just that long ago?

Soon after, long, big, straight trees had been harvested from the forest nearby. The chopping sounds echoed through the forest on some days. All for the great hall. A number of men, along with our animals, were commanded to help with getting the logs to the site, including da. Even from this distance, I can tell that it is a mammoth building. A building that size, with that many trees, doesn't go up quickly. I wonder if it will be finished this year.

Shifting my gaze, I can see that the garden has weeds. At least, I can pride myself on the fact that while I tended the garden, there were few, if any weeds. I'll be helping the garden actually, taking away rooted shoots before they get bigger and that would clog up the paths between the rows of plants if not removed now. Thinning and pruning is always good for growth.

In my mind's eye, I see ma picking certain plants, picking just the tips, the newest growth, for a specific need, placing the leaves into her pestle. Her real magick was knowing the plants well enough that she could determine an imagined outcome or close enough to it that she could tweak it, achieving results desired. My experience even now doesn't match hers, but maybe by experimenting through the winter, through this pregnancy, I'll have gained much by next spring But practice on whom? Wild life? Do I have a choice?

As I wait, I almost wish ma to enter the garden. I decide, however, that as much as I want to see her, I'm better off not. Seeing her will only make me angry, an emotion I'd rather escape. What's best for me is to have nothing to do with her, with them. As I sit waiting and watching, I convince myself that I am entitled to a portion of what I supplied and contributed to their existence during my life there. I'm not stealing anything; I'm owed. I deserve whatever I take.

On the morning of the next day, I wonder if my watch is folly. I begin to wonder if I'm wasting my time here when I could have been hunting and gathering food. But with what? The tools I need to become an efficient hunter are here, not back at the cave. No, I am not wasting time. I need to be patient. I need to wait for the weather that will be my cover.

My lower back aches from lack of movement. I have to urinate more frequently than I like, which I blame on the baby. To do so, I have to trek far enough away so as not to leave a scent of my hideout. If I can detect animals who have urinated in the forest, surely the best of hunters would be able to detect my urine. I can't do anything that draws attention to this area.

As I watch the village and the people, I realize that they are preparing for Midsummer celebration. If true to tradition, they should be leaving tonight to celebrate in Hrothgar's village. Maybe even at the location of the unfinished structure of Heorot.

Only a few will stay behind: the sick, women about to give birth or those who already just did, and the elders who no longer can travel. At the same time, chances are high in my favor that these few will not venture outside, especially during the dark of night. The moon will be full tonight, a good omen when it conjoins the celebration of season. The veil of Other will be thin tonight, though it is always the thinnest during the harvest season at the end of October.

The morning moves slowly. I see the earl, their honorable leader isolate a young girl behind a shed and lift her skirts, groping, with her struggling to get away. My emotions rise. Memories fill me. I want to scream. But I know the screaming will do no good. It didn't then and it won't now.

I hate this feeling. I don't like losing control. My breathing is shallow and too fast, so I force myself to inhale deeply, sending a calming column down my spine, and then slowly blowing out the stress.

When the girl finally escapes, the earl merely laughs. If I despised men before, my hatred of them grows now. That girl looked to be only seven or eight. While no child is wholly innocent regarding procreation, we are—were innocent of the act itself, but now I wonder if it was just me who was the innocent. I wonder how many children in the village know more through no fault of their own, but say nothing. Like I had done.

I watch my brothers wrestle with each other as they perform chores, feeding animals, pitching old straw with a fork from the barn portion of the house into a small wagon to be moved and dumped next to the garden and fields to spread later, waiting for the final furrow for the upcoming winter, when the field will be harvested and empty of grain. Already, I can see that the grasses have been cut, piled, and are drying, waiting to be transported into the barn.

In the trees and bushes, I watch older birds caring for younger birds, fledglings that have flown from the safety of their nest but aren't quite able to feed themselves fully yet. They cry for food and parents oblige with bug or seed. I watch the youngsters forage, mimicking their parents' hunting skills, but pretend weakness when the parents are nearby. When winter comes, the young will be fully on their own, their parents no longer helping them sustain their diet. They'll be on their own to live or die.

The trees are thick in green, but in another few months, they will be bare. A few leaves will hang on tightly unwilling to be let loose, to wither and die on the wind. The evergreens that stay green in winter already function as a refuge for smaller birds flittering in and out of the pine needles, seeking shelter from birds of prey. The evergreens secret me from view, as well. Were I to be discovered, I would be preyed upon again, only this time my death would be assured.

Suddenly, ma appears, rushing out of the house. Re-pinning her hair, she washes her hands at the basin. These two actions are the last things she does before going anywhere.

I sit up and peer through the evergreens for a better view of the houses. Sure enough, other families are exiting their homes with the usual baskets, lanterns, blankets, and anything they need for the long evening ahead.

As I sit, waiting for darkness and clouds to cover the moon, I admit that tonight is going to be long. Not only has my patience been worn thin as I waited, but before I return to my cave, I'll have to replant these shoots, quickly, while the moon is still full. One thing I know from time spent in ma's garden is that anything planted in a waning moon will sit there until the new and waxing moon.

Shadows on the ground begin to disappear and the darkness that fades shadows into the landscape allows me to rise and move forward. If anyone happens to step outside the house, they won't see me unless I step on a twig or make any other noise not akin to the sounds of the night.

While it's warm out tonight and the best time to be thinning out a garden, not to mention replanting the shoots, there are only a few weeks left for these shoots to re-establish themselves before the first frost occurs. I will need to cover them thickly with leaves and pine needles, at that time, so that they will survive the winter, but, that's a chore I'll think about later.

A few villagers will return later tonight, walking home under the full moon. Most will stay, sleeping in the open meadow. Ultimately, the weather will dictate their choices. This will be the first year that I won't be attending.

I can't think about what I am missing.

Instead, I need to remember everything I must collect and need to steal. By the time anyone returns, I plan on being gone.

I can't fool myself thinking that I am borrowing. I have no intention of returning anything I take. Besides, they deserve to lose far more than what little bits of pieces of their life that will hardly be missed tomorrow. If anything, they'll blame someone in the family or a greedy neighbor for the theft. So much for a loving community.

As a safety measure, I spit on the ground several times, then take the wet soil and rub it on my face, neck, and any skin that became exposed during my three-day wait. My wish is that I'll be invisible just by thinking it so. But just in case . . .

I slink my way toward the garden. Once there, I move into the garden, feeling confident that if I stay toward the back, the bigger plants will hide me. Just in case, I keep low. Without wasting time, I pull up the smaller shoots, mechanically placing them in a pile at the end of the row. Silently and stealthily, I move quickly from row to row. Soon, many small piles await final pickup, each at the end of a row. Done, I retrieve the two deer hooves. I imprint the earth where I've been with hoof marks in haphazard patterns so that it looks like many deer were here. In the process, I also trample some of the plants with the hoofs. It has to look as if Nature's animals maundered through the garden, eating, and looking for green morsels. What few berries are here, I snatch and eat, thoroughly trampling those plants with the hoofs. I need to create realism. If I'm lucky, ma will not discover anything amiss. At least, nothing out of the ordinary. Far too often, ma and I would find hoof prints in the garden, so this invasion won't be new for her.

I move into the village itself, my heart racing. Quickly, I sneak into my old home and take my mother's favorite blanket, a blanket I always coveted for its warmth. Not only do I need cloth to cover myself with at night until I can kill and create my own furs for clothing and bedding, I need something that allows me to tote back my booty. The blanket will serve as a sack.

Since ma never favored me, let her blame one of her sons or da. Knowing her as I do, she'll blame another woman and no doubt will bully and press her way into their homes, looking for it. I take a worthy axe and hoe that belong to the meanest man in the village.

I take sewing materials from the best seamstress. I have no choice, but I'm not greedy. I take only those items she won't miss, since she has an abundant supply of needles and threads. I'm almost at the door when I hear a noise.

Someone walks slowly toward the door.

I dart into the darkest corner.

I disappear into the shadows, making myself invisible.

The door creaks open.

It's the seamstress herself, a woman far older than ma. She's both thin and of little height. Bent over, she moves slowly, as if in pain.

I hold my breath, hoping that she won't come to the fire to stir the ashes and coals or to put more wood on it.

My heart beats loudly to my ears.

I will her to move past the fire pit and move toward the back of the room and her bed. She pauses at the fire, but then shakes her head. As she shuffles toward the back of the room, I move quickly. Staying low, I'm at the door and out before she reaches her bed. I take a chance by not looking out first. I have no choice. I can't be trapped inside. Outside the door, if I'm seen, I can escape more easily.

I realize how risky my actions are, but, again, I have no choice. I won't survive without these tools.

Hunkered down in the shadows of one house, I look around to make sure no one else is outside the houses. All appears clear.

I continue my thievery. I take meat and fruit from the best cook. Since so many give her food for her services, how can she miss what little I've taken? It's only enough to give me strength for my own hunting.

I don't hesitate to take a good supply of knifes and tanning tools, a little from everyone, but I take the best knife from the forge maker. He has so many. I'm hoping no one will miss what I'm taking tonight. All except ma. She'll notice right away, and she'll be furious. Taking her blanket is stupid really, but I don't care. I want her to want something back so badly that she suffers. She'll find a way to take it out on the family.

My arms full, I scamper back to the big rock and my cover for the past couple days. I dump everything on the ground. A good night's work. Mentally, I go through my list to make sure I haven't forgotten anything.

I spread out the blanket, packing one pot with the plants. I place the sewing materials and other smaller items in the second pot, including any of the smaller, sharp objects. I lay the bulk of the bigger tools between the two pots and then bring up two opposite corners of the blanket and tie them together. Then I bring the other two opposite corners together and tie them. I weave a hoe handle through these tied corners until the blanket corners rest up against the hoe itself. I heave the blanket carefully and slowly around, onto my back, with the hoe's handle and the corners now on my shoulder, holding the handle against my body. In my other hand, the axe.

My muscles will ache by the time I reach home, but I'll be glad of this raid later. These plants will aid me in the birth and even later for cuts, bites, illnesses, and any injuries.

Definitely a good night's work, but there is more work to be done before the night is over.

I look back at the houses, the smoke coming out of the chimneys, the thin strips of light that filter out of the cracks around the doors and in the walls. While they have gone to bed or to the celebration believing they are safe, I am out here, taking what I want. I could have taken so much more.

If I ever had any doubts before about wanting to be a part of this community, I have no longings anymore. In fact, I feel nothing for them, not even the slightest loathing. While I may have earlier thought that I was stealing from them, I now realize that all and anything belongs to the victor who can take it and hold on to it.

Moving out of my hiding spot, I look back one more time and realize that they have no idea what they have created and fear the most: a monster in their midst.

As much as I want to destroy their homes, their lives, I turn toward my home, knowing leaving everything the same is best. I don't want to create suspicion, should I need to return. I want them to think they are safe and secure. As I pass by the dragon stake, the place where this new life of mine began, I consider taking the axe and chopping it down. Again, I don't want them to know that someone was in their midst. Someday, I'll bring it down. For now, I need my strength for the return trip home and the planting I need to accomplish before tomorrow's light.

* * *

The days of summer pass too quickly. The plants I obtained from ma's garden flourish in that small, but well-protected area surrounded by rocks that not only creates a high fence that even the tallest of men can't see over but the rocks create heat so that the ground is warmer than the ground outside of those rocks. I couldn't have picked a more ideal place. Plus, the only opening into the area is secreted within a maze of more rocks.

The dragon has been true to her word, leaving me wood, which I move into my part of the cave, chopping it there so that it will fit within my fire pit. I nearly didn't take the axe in my steal, but I'm glad I did. Even though I'm not using it in the forest, I use it in here both on my kills, chopping the meat into manageable sizes, and on the wood, too. Actually, I feel quite clever discovering chopping meat with a big axe making the work easy. Men use small hammer-like axes and large knifes but I've never seen bones split via my method. As a result, I'm able to easily reach the nutritious bone marrow right away, either by sucking it out or cooking the bone in water, creating a blood broth basis for meat stew. I feel more alive and energetic than I ever did in the village. Probably because I'm getting the richest cuts of meats now, including all the organ meats.

The baby kicks a lot these days and my belly is sticking out. It's almost as if the baby is turning somersaults. Every now and then, I can see the outline of a tiny foot kicking out, an imprint on my stomach. It doesn't feel like my body is changing much until the day I wake up and notice that I can't see my feet anymore when standing. Right now, I can stretch my neck out and see my toes, but I know in another month or so, even that feat will be impossible.

* * *

One day slides into another, the hot days of August ease all too quickly into shorter days and longer, cooler nights of September. My skills have sharpened. I feel stronger and leaner despite my belly that more resembles a small boulder under my skin.

My days are routine. In the evening, I place a pot under the small but constant trickle of water that falls on the back wall in my cave and put it on the coals to heat up. Depending on what herbs I have available, I make tea: lavender, dandelion, or bark. I breakfast on whatever food I gathered the day before or have cooked earlier in the week and am still feasting on. A deer can last several weeks, so I've learned to smoke more than I eat to store for the upcoming, long winter season when I won't be able to get out as I get closer to birthing or the time afterward when I won't want to be leaving the cave.

Then I move wood, a daily necessity, if I want to keep the fire alive. Usually, after a half dozen trips, I'll stop. I need to reserve energy for my outside treks to find food, herbs, or items I can use as tools, like bones, rocks, and discarded carcasses. I use these as bait for bigger prey that I can't kill outright, such as a wolf or bear. Instead, I lace the carcass with poisonous herbs. While the herbs kill my prey, as long as I can get my kill quickly and gut it, the poison doesn't spread into the meat that I eat. While I dislike having to discard organ meat, bleeding it out so other animals don't eat the poison, I'm glad to have these large, warm pelts. I don't need many, so the poisoning will stop when my minimum needs are met.

Today I'm hunting, so most of my day will be spent around this one activity. As usual, I hike several miles to the south and west until I'm far enough away from my home and all other communities. I wonder if I'll be able to travel this distance as my belly expands and my energy wanes. I remember how village women would complain how tired they became as the birthing day grew closer. Out in the wild, though, I notice that the animals continue as usual. The pregnant deer stay with the herd until they're ready to give birth. Only then, the doe goes off alone for a week or so before returning to the herd with her baby or twins.

I resolve that I need to be more like the animals in the wild than the simpering weak-minded village women. Maybe this is what my mother was talking about when she called these pregnant women lazy. Ma never slowed down now that I think about it. Was it just her nature, or was it a mindset? I wonder, too, how much da played a part of her having to get up right away from the birthing bed. Did she just learn to adjust and never complain or was giving birth so natural for her that her energy was never spent?

I decide that it was probably a mixture of both.

When I lie on the outside grasses at night and look into the night, the vastness of space and stars astounds me. I contemplate my life and my existence—our existence—endlessly. I feel so small in the expanse of space and time. How important can my life be in this enormous universe? How much of it am I not seeing?

And then, my thoughts return to my immediate world, and I ponder about the living creatures on this earth and realize that we're all doing the same: eating, sleeping, raising families, moving through life with no real end goal. In the end, we all die. No one, nothing survives.

Why do we hang onto existence so tightly when the end result is the same? Why stall the inevitable? As if in answer to my question, the baby kicks. I rub the spot with my hand, both in a soothing motion but also hoping I will feel more movement with my hand. I realize that the baby has answered my question. We hang on for our children. Will I feel different as my baby grows, eventually leaving the nest, much as I watch birds desert their young once the chicks are able to fend for themselves? Or, will I be one of those parents, such as I saw in the village, like my parents, where I meddle, never leaving my child alone even though he or she is fully capable without me? Only time will tell.

For now, I have chores to do, and I welcome them. These chores remind me every day that I'm free to live as I choose. Honestly, if I have a day where I don't want to perform these chores, I can disregard them for the day or two. But in reality, they are a daily necessity. Initially, while I disliked the burden of these chores, I am content with the ritual and the freedom they provide. What would I do without these chores? Wander aimlessly through the landscape, biding time until my non-existence?

I'm sure, in the future, as I recover from this impending birth and other unexpected events, there will be times that I'm unable to perform or move around as desired, but again, it will be a decision that I make, not decisions impressed upon me, with an emphasis of someone else saying they know what's best for me.

Every day I move wood and stop after half a dozen trips. Today, I decide to move as much as I can without tiring. I want to continue to build up my strength and get ahead for that time this winter when I'm incapacitated and cave bound.

Suddenly, I have an image of a toddler or crawling baby and see them falling into the mere, drowning. I have no siblings or other adults around to help me in the raising of this child. Its safety will be my responsibility alone. In fact, there will never be assistance for me This baby will not have a community of any kind to learn from or have a community that will look out for his or her best interest. There will only be me. My health, my ability will always be tested in good times and in bad. I'll have to be resilient and hope I'm able to gain his or her cooperation far sooner than my parents were able to get that from their children. While I didn't have any sisters, I noticed those families with women had cleaner clothes, cleaner homes, better food. Da and my brothers never suffered because of any lack of work on my part or ma's. The two of us managed okay despite being outnumbered. I did notice that other families who lacked female siblings suffered more in their appearances and household upkeep than we did. And, those families with no mother, well, that's why my marriage to Angus had been so important. With no woman, life was all the more difficult for a family.

Equally so, a household with no man suffers, too, but at least others helped by providing meat now and then. Not so with a womanless household. No woman comes to help with the cleaning or the meals. The children are expected to do those chores.

Nor do I want to run ragged because of a disobedient child. I begin to wonder if I'll be able to spy on this child, becoming invisible when needed. Yes, this skill requires development if I'm to survive well. I want to become such a great expert that I am feared. Respected. Like ma.

Do you hear yourself? Ironically, I realize that I am becoming one of those adults who presumes to know better than the child. But a toddler is different from a teenager. Isn't it? If I say yes, then I'm saying my parents were right in telling me what to do, though I always knew better.

I'm not sure I want to face these conflicting thoughts. I don't want to believe that my parents were right. That would mean that I was wrong. How could I be wrong, when they were my feelings, my beliefs? How can my feelings have been wrong when I feel—

Instantly, I'm aware that I've not thought about how I feel in a long time. I've been existing. Though I have been safe, far safer than ever imagined when this solo journey first began. As I consider where I exist today both physically, emotionally, and spiritually, I realize I am happy. I'm young, healthy—though if I had my preference I wouldn't be pregnant. Since I can't change that fact, I accept it without reservation despite how the pregnancy occurred. Also, I'm not hungry anymore. Something I can't remember ever happening before. As long as I can remember, I've been hungry, never able to get enough food. I'm taking care of myself fairly well, and I'm one with Nature, far more than I ever thought I could be.

I feel Her moods, hear the chatter of the animals, those in the air, on the land, and down beneath the soil. I sense the feelings of the plants, big and small, and pay my respects to them all, every day when I am within their presence. I do not take their attributes, their feelings lightly. Just as I am to serve, so do they.

In that moment, I realize that my serving has not always been in the right spirit when it came to family. I always performed the duties, but not always willingly. Not when my freedom felt squashed, flattened to near oblivion. I have true freedom today, and I refuse to give it up now that I'm acclimated and thriving. I feel angry just thinking that someone could try, would take my freedom away if they were to discover my existence.

I stop at a small pond, merely a dip in the landscape with some pooled water, for a drink. The surface of the water is still and as I bend over, I see my reflection. The last time I saw myself was in the wash bowl at my parent's house. The difference between that time and now is stark. Then my hair was long and neatly braided, my face clean and white, my face expressionless. It was as if I had no soul and I could see through myself. Now my hair is askew, usually in my face, and my face muddy in color. Dark from the sun but darker from dirt that doesn't wash off completely despite my swims into and from the cave through the mere. I don't think of cleanliness anymore, not the way I used to. I left that other girl behind. Now my eyes sparkle and I truly see myself. This image isn't lifeless like that earlier reflection.

Finally, at a favorite location to hunt, I settle into my wait until dusk when the deer will be moving. While I wait, I scour my surroundings for animal footprints and for herbs or flowers that I can dry and add to my medicine cache. Even though I've stretched a line, made of twisted vines, across the smallest part of the cave and near the fire to hang plants for drying, the drying takes twice as long as it did when I lived in the house. The humidity is high in the cave, which is the main reason for my fire, even in summer. Even though I know the cave maintains a constant temperature, in summer, the cave is cool. In winter, while the cave may be warmer than outside temperatures, it will be bone-chilling cold because of the same humidity.

* * *

As the weeks progress, my skills improve and the work I perform follows one task after another, one day after another, one week following another. Before I know it, December is here. The shortest day is not far away, based on the sun's position in the sky upon rising and setting. The stars reveal the winter constellations and I'm reminded of their individual stories that I used to hear around the fire.

My belly, while not as huge as some women I'd seen, is large. Walking is more difficult. I feel myself waddling, much like the occasional duck that lands in the mere. I can feel that the baby is in its birthing position and kicks and moves as if trying to get out. At times, I can see a foot pushing out, its print upon my belly for a second or two before it disappears. Other times, I can see the sharp poke of an elbow as it moves or turns around against my belly, and then it, too, disappears. An active baby, for sure. As much as I want it out so I can be comfortable again, I know that comfort will never be the same again. I will be dealing with other kinds of discomforts.

I'm in my final month. While the pregnancy wears on me, not allowing me to perform certain chores the same way, what I don't like is that my energy level doesn't stay high anymore. There are times in the day when I'm so weary I can't think. I'm there right now.

I am out gathering the last of any berries I can find. I have them wrapped up in my basket—my old dress that is thin and only good as a toting device. I approach the mere wishing I could see my feet. I sit at the mere's edge for a moment, putting my feet into the water. My ankles are swollen, something I need to watch as I finish this pregnancy.

Once the flies and mosquitoes start finding their way through the cracks of my muddied skin, I slide into the mere, the dress with berries in hand and toss my braid, which has many loose tendrils onto my back with the other. I'm close to the edge of one of the dirt banks rather than in the middle as would occur had I jumped in. Underwater, I turn to swim toward the rock wall.

My head is jerked back. My hair pulled!

I panic, wondering who has me by my hair.

I twist around.

No one is there.

And then, I notice, my hair is caught on a submerged limb. I try to pull myself free. I can't.

I struggle. I entangle myself more.

I want to breathe. But I can't. I'm stuck here, trapped underwater.

Instantly, I let go of the berries and follow my braid from my head to where the hair is tangled.

I yank and pull. I try to ignore the shooting pain in my head.

I need air. I struggle to rise to the surface but can't make it. I breathe, only it's water.

I gag, expelling it and struggle not to inhale.

I can't die here! Not like this! I grab the offending twig and yank it from the branch.

I kick my legs and surface, gasping, coughing, and spitting. I push back the hair from my face, angry.

The berries are gone.

The entire venture outside the cave today is now a waste.

I move the braid, now more loose hair than braid, along with the offending twig back behind me.

This time I dive straight for the middle. Seconds later, I'm in the cave. I climb out and head straight for a knife that's by the fire. I start cutting off my hair.

I yank it and slice. Grab it and slice. Handful after handful, I toss my hair into the fire where it sizzles, smells, and burns quickly.

When I think I'm done, I run my hand over my head. My head feels naked, yet blissfully free. I notice the chill in the cave more, too. My hair is short, probably no more than an inch or two all around. It feels spikey. I smile.

I decide that I'll never have long hair again. It's a curse, a weakness, plus the sign of a woman. I'm not a woman. I just am.

* * *

A week later, when I exit the cave, the air is much colder and the ground is white with snow. It is only the third time in my life that I have seen snow. It never stays more than a couple days and there never has been an accumulation. Just enough snow that tracking and hunting is made easier, I used to hear my brothers say.

Anticipating a need for dry fur, I have hidden such a cloak deep in nearby bushes. It is a sacrifice of my safety to hide it as I have, but coming out of the water into this freezing temperature can be life threatening. I am hardened to the cold, but I still need to be careful. As a result, I leave my clothing in the cave and come out of the water naked, so that my clothing wouldn't be soaked. In fact, I have been doing this for the past month once the temperatures started dropping.

Once I am covered and warmth returns, I consider lying on the ground and making a snow angel like I used to do with my brothers.

To do so will leave marks, which wouldn't be wise. As I stand there, I look at my prints coming from the mere to where I stand. I don't like that I am leaving a trail, so I get a branch with leaves and brush away my prints.

I need to find food.

During the last week, my belly felt like it was stretching and becoming harder. I know my time is approaching, but I feel safe enough to leave the cave for this excursion. A pig will last for weeks and keep me from having to dig into the smoked meat I have preserved and stored in the cave. I don't want to disturb that store of food until I have no other choice. I know that the store will feed me for a good number of weeks, if not several months if I'm careful, but I am reluctant to touch it until absolutely needed. Certainly, I can't keep it forever, but I'm mindful of how little I'll be able to leave the cave for a few months after the baby is here.

Is it wise to venture into the woods, though, and leave a trail? Glancing toward where the heavy-wooded terrain begins, I can see that there is no snow there. With a light dusting out here, I use the branch again and sweep away my footprints.

Once I reach the trees, seeing that my steps no longer exist, I drop the branch, prepared to use it again upon my return. In fact, I should return the branch to its prior location. I try to keep Nature around the mere as untouched as possible.

As I move deeper into the woods, I feel my belly tighten. It is starting. Maybe. As a new mother, I figure I have a few hours before needing to be back if this is indeed the start of labor. Besides, this one tightening doesn't mean much right now.

I decide this time that I will hunt close to the mere's proximity, just in case. Walking away from the mere for about an hour is far enough. As I walk to what I think will be a good position, I experience several more contractions, but they are light. I judge them to be about fifteen minutes apart right now. I'm definitely in labor.

I get lucky. I hear a pig grunting close by. Judging by the noise— leaves rustling and soft grunts—I determine that it is rooting in the ground, looking for truffles and other food. So far, it isn't aware of my presence. I relax, shifting into invisible mode, my spear at the ready. The fewer movements I make as it comes closer to me, the better. I will it to come closer. I continue that thought process, and then suddenly, I have a glimpse of it. Thankfully, it isn't a large boar. It's a young pig, almost grown, probably born in the spring.

I watch, silent despite the hardening of my belly as another contraction is upon me. I know holding my breath will make the pain more intense, so I breathe quietly, blowing out and mentally blowing out the pain with the breath. The pig moves closer. Finally, the contraction stops. As it moves closer still, I hold my breath . . . waiting.

The pig turns. I throw my spear. It hits right where I aimed—its heart. It squeals loudly, takes a couple steps and drops. I get up from my kneeling position where I was hiding in the tall grass, moving far slower than I want. My huge belly makes me awkward and slower than I like. I gasp as my belly tightens, again. Mentally, I count. Finally, the muscles relax. I need to hurry.

Nearly at the pig, I walk around it so that its back is to me, just in case it is still alive. If it was to get up, it would not be facing me. I grab the top of the spear that stands straight up to the sky and wiggle it, so I can see the belly . . . a female. She is dead.

Good. I don't want to have to stab her again. Slowly, I drop to my knees and pull out my knife. In just a few minutes, I have her disemboweled, dressed as much as I can perform in the shortest of time. The dressing is sloppy compared to my usual precise cuts, but I don't care. Time is my priority, right now. I am initially saddened to discover she's pregnant, but the reality is that it is either her or me; otherwise, I'd have no food for the next couple of weeks. Normally, when I see a pregnant pig, I leave her alone, to live another day, but there wasn't any sign she was pregnant. The piglets are barely formed. Normally, I would take the whole pig back to the cave and gut it there. Nothing is ever wasted. Today isn't a normal day, though. I need to get back to the cave quickly and I can't carry a whole pig with its innards today. I stand up and gasp.

The realization of what is happening hits me hard. When did I allow this child to enslave my future? To reduce me to hunting in the freezing cold like this, to put all my creature comforts aside? That's a laugh. When was the last time I had a real creature comfort? When I suckled at my mother's breast, perhaps?

Another pain clenches my middle, creating a new kind of tightness. I make myself breathe through the pain, having nothing to lean on, to grab hold of. The spear lies on the ground. Finally, the pain lessens. I retrieve the spear and walk over to the nearest tree, leaning the spear against the trunk. I retrace my steps, bending over as best I can, grabbing the pig's hind legs. I lift her over my shoulder awkwardly, not liking that I can't maneuver her around my neck as I would have done normally. I do the best I can.

I grab the spear and head for the cave. Far too soon, I feel the burning in my back and shoulder muscles begin. Fortunately, I'm not far from my destination.

The pains remind me just how alive I am and the life I am about to give. The thing I fear most, the only future I have now, a reminder of the past and the event that ruined my once idyllic and happy life, coalesces into the round belly that tightens harder this time, catching me off guard.

Instinctively, I catch my breath. I try to relax, laughing at the thought that my other life had been idyllic.

The night will be long, and I will be exhausted by night's end for my work has only begun. Finally, I'm at the mere's edge. Quickly, I drop the pig and strip, hiding the fur, placing it out of sight but where it will remain dry.

I grab the pig's hind legs again. Taking a deep breath, I jump into the water, the pig in one hand, the spear in the other. Rather than feeling fat and clumsy, now I am buoyant with better flexibility. Because I've performed this task multiple times, I don't have to think about it.

Quickly, I swim the distance, diving deep down, then beneath the rock, and then back up and into the cave, until I can feel the cave floor ledge under my feet. Fortunately, for me, this underwater ledge allows me to stand and toss the pig up onto the dry floor in front of me. I toss the spear forward and start climbing, eventually rolling onto the cave floor as my strength wanes.

My teeth clatter and I shiver. I grab a fur and start rubbing myself dry. Another contraction stops me, forcing me to wait and endure its presence. The contractions are getting longer and more intense.

I want to call out, but I can't just in case anyone could hear my cry. Sound carries more easily in the winter where there are no leaves and bushes outside to buffer the noise. I have to hurry.

The meat needs attention. Methodically, I cut off a hock, skewer it on a sharpened stick, and then place it on a spit over the fire. Too tired to cut up the meat and smoke it, I half carry, half drag the rest of the carcass to the small cold room for storage. The meat will stay cool and protected from most all predators. I'm careful not to touch any of the spider webs nearby as they help keep the smallest of prey—the pesky fly—from finding the meat.

Back in the main room, I grab my clothes, but decide against them. I won't need clothes tonight. A tanned skin—one of my first— that serves as a blanket will suffice. Tired to the core, I sink down on the skins. A contraction comes and goes. Several more follow.

The low fire, rich with coals, creates shadows that flicker on the cave's walls and, like stars in the sky, dots of sparkling light showcase minerals peppered throughout the rocky walls.

Time moves slowly as my belly continually tightens and loosens, like a strong clamp of Nature's hand.

My water breaks. I wish it to be a sign that the end is close. But, the contractions continue. I have to throw more wood on the fire. The pain radiating from my hips is unbearable. I find myself holding my breath and having to force myself to breathe.

Finally, I want to bear down. I feel the babe moving down. And then, I feel its head appearing between my legs. The skull isn't soft like I've felt before in other births. Instead, it feels hard and unmoving. I panic not knowing what is happening.

I hear my mother's voice, just as she would tell others to blow out and relax, to take deep breaths and focus on the baby, not the pain.

I follow her instructions. I bear down when the contractions begin and then breathe properly when it ends, waiting for the next one to begin. I want to push between contractions, but again I hear ma's voice, saying to wait, otherwise tearing can occur.

I want to cry, I'm so tired.

My hands feel the head coming out when I push down, but then it retracts again when the pain ends. Will this baby ever be born, or will I die here amid pain and contractions? A head between my thighs?

I'm determined that I will not die. Not by this baby and certainly by no other. No man will ever touch me again.

With the next contraction, I bear down hard, harder than before, and I don't stop even when the contraction ends. I know I'm risking being torn by doing so, but I don't care. I just want this thing out of me!

The head emerges.

I'm barely able to catch my breath. Another contraction closely follows.

The body slides out easily.

I rise, leaning on one elbow, more exhausted than I've ever been in my life. A large lump that more resembles a pile of a gutted pig lies at the apex of my legs. The pile is still. A male. I sit up, expecting to feel pain but realizing I'm more numb than in pain. In short time, the pain will come. For now, I'm relieved. At least I can tend to business. Lightly, I tug the umbilical cord, careful not to tear it away from the mass that still needs to exit my body, nor tear it from the lump in front of me.

I tug on the boy and look for movement, but there is none. I want to be glad that he will not suffer through this life alone with only me as a companion, but find myself strangely sad. My mind muddles. Do I take care of him first or me? Without me, he'll surely die, but if he doesn't cry soon, he'll die anyway. I tug on the cord with one hand, a cord that is now pale and disappears into my body and still connects me to the baby, and shake him with the other. The afterbirth slides out of my body. I continue shaking the baby. With one hand, I wipe myself with the moss I have piled beside me, then pack a substantial amount between my legs, wrapping myself in the worst of the skins I've collected, so that the discharge will soak into it. Soon, this skin will be soaked and required a good rinsing. I'll have no choice but to wash the skins in the mere.

I look at the baby. A baby. My baby. How long has it been since it first appeared? Less than a minute? A minute? Two? More?

Suddenly, I realize how pale it is. Blank eyes stare up at me. It has a little nub of a nose, broader and flatter than normal with tiny openings, and a slash of a mouth. The jaw is wider and larger than normal. One arm is shorter than the other. One leg is twisted. Then suddenly, its arm moves. Startled, I instinctively jerk away, then reach out. To do what? What would ma do? Should I let it die? It's obviously deformed and so ugly. Would death be a kindness? But if it does die, then I'll be alone.

Truly alone.

The whole body twitches, then moves as if struggling. I scoop it up, dig my finger into its mouth, sweeping my finger from one side to the other, pulling out the mucus that plugs its mouth. I turn it over and start smacking it solidly on its back, between the shoulders, then down further, repeating the motions. Motions I've seen my mother perform.

In this moment, I realize it is as innocent as me, caught in a storm of events not of its own making.

Did I let it lie there too long without attention? To punish it, to let it die is doing the same thing that society did to me. This little boy, even if disgusting in appearance, is caught in a situation not of its making.

I clean him off. His head is huge, larger than other newborns that I've seen. His face doesn't look natural, like other newborns, but I can't determine what is wrong. I've never seen a face such as his, except that night. That horrible night that was his conception. The baby's limbs appear average even though one arm is shorter than the other. His body is tiny. Will he even survive his first winter?

If no one else is going to love it, who am I to join them and make a disastrous situation even worse? This poor child is without normalcy, has a broken body in parents, community, and environment. No, not in environment, for this environment is ours. It is our strength, our will. We will survive.

He mews like a kitten. I pick him up and put him to my breast. Immediately, he suckles, greedily, as if he's been waiting his entire existence for this. I am his lifeblood, his connection to survival and continuance. My life as I know it is forever changed and is merged to this small pitiful creature through no fault of his own, bears the horrors of his conception, his sire.

* * *

I wake up, startled. I have no idea why. Then, I hear the baby crying. I don't remember going to sleep. The baby is next to me on the fur, uncovered, as am I. Was I so exhausted that I fell asleep with him crying? No, I remember that he fell asleep, and I lay down for a minute, thinking I should stir the fire.

The crying gets louder. Suddenly, there's a strange sensation in my breasts, as if they are filling up and yet falling. I offer him a breast, and he feeds hungrily. I find his feeding makes the one breast feel better, so after a while, I switch him to the other, hoping that breast will feel better, too.

While he nurses, I look to the fire and am relieved to see a few coals smoldering. Never has that fire gone out since the dragon gave me fire. How dangerous would it be for it to go out now, with a new baby needing the heat far more than I do? Now that he's finished, I get up and grimace at the sudden flood of blood that streams down both thighs. The moss is saturated. I cover the baby with a corner of the fur we lie on. I throw wood on the coals. Fortunately, the wood is dry and catches quickly.

I want to lie down again but jump into the mere, instead. I knew it would be cold and it is. I wake up, wishing there was a better way to clean myself of this blood, but there isn't. This is the fastest way. I leave the bloodied moss behind in the water as I climb out. Quickly, I grab a handful of clean moss and hope for the best. I have no idea how long I'll bleed. I never talked about these matters with ma. Nor do I recall hearing other women talk. I'm completely on my own here. I can only guess. With only a few months' worth of experience of monthly menses behind me, even they were not consistent or long enduring. Not as I heard others complain. Maybe I was just fortunate. Maybe I will be fortunate here too. I have no idea. If those monthly events only lasted a few days, how long does one bleed after a birth?

The baby whimpers. I sit down next to him and uncover him. At that moment, he pees, urine arching high and landing on me. I place my hand over the spray, which results in it splashing all over him. He jerks and cries at a fevered pitch. All his limbs are thrashing. I wipe him down as best I can and pick him up. Automatically, he turns and begins trying to suck at my skin again. I adjust him so that he can find my nipple, which he does easily enough. The silence is immediate.

What a difference between the crying and the suckling silence. I feel myself relaxing in the quiet.

I have no idea when I grew accustomed to the silence. I guess now I will become acclimated to noise again. Truthfully, though, I hope the noise is minimal. I remember the dragon speaking about noise when I first discovered the cave and not wanting any noise to make known our whereabouts. Or cause her discomfort.

I'm mindful of his every cry and do whatever I can to quiet him quickly.

Suddenly, I feel overwhelmed, overcome with emotion unlike I have ever experienced before. The baby is only a day old, nearly two, and I'm so exhausted already. How will I ever endure? How long before I feel like myself again?

* * *

The next day continues in monotonous torture. I never realized that taking care of a baby was so draining. Thinking back when I used to care for my siblings, I realize now that I wasn't responsible for them hour upon hour but rather in short durations when ma was needed elsewhere. Even then, my brothers weren't babies. They were walking and talking, feeding themselves, and playing with each other. I wasn't taking care of them as much as simply keeping an eye on them.

Now the responsibility is all mine. Every minute of the day. And all night long, too. Already exhausted, I want to be outside for a while by myself. Do I dare leave him alone for a minute? Is it possible that I can take him outside with me? In time, I will have no choice. I'll have to take him with me. Can he hold his breath underwater to get outside? And, if he does survive that swim, how will he stay warm outside?

Thinking it through, I realize that I will be carrying him, but it has to be in such a way that my hands are free. I'll have to create some kind of apparatus that allows me to carry him on my back for most of the time or on my stomach in such a way that he can nurse while I walk or hunt. How is it I never saw such a contraption in the village? Probably because there were other people—siblings, a visiting aunt—to watch the baby.

I have meat enough, clean water, and firewood, but how long before I need to venture out into the forest again? Truthfully, I miss not being able to go out.

I realize my thoughts are spinning in circles since I'm back to wondering how I can take him with me when I do venture outside again. I decide it will have to be soon or I'll go crazy. I have no choice but to take him with me. I can't leave him in the cave to cry for hours and take the chance that he will disturb the dragon who has every right to ask me to leave.

I feel safe here. I don't want to leave.

So, instead, I'll endure.

As I look at him, I realize that he needs a name. The size of his head, to me, already shows strength. Despite his small body size right now, he has strength in his struggle to survive, too. Strengel. No, I don't like it. He is born of a giant, a monster, with a face like an animal. Grendel.

Now that I look at him, his face doesn't remind me of that shadowed face hovering above me. Instead of a huge monster, I'm looking at a small cub. He doesn't look like any of the other babies in the village or resemble any of my younger brothers when they were born either. No, he looks totally different. I shudder to think he could grow up looking like his father . . . a huge monster. No, it can't happen. I won't let it.

* * *

The next few days are pure torture. Giving birth was easy compared to how tired I am at doing nothing all day. I'm unable to put the baby down without him screaming, so I carry him everywhere, while I perform any and every task. All of them. I can do only a little in a day because of the length of time it takes me to complete each task.

I'm only able to move one piece of wood at a time from the pile to the fire, so rather than one trip with an armful of wood, I'm making several. Even then, I can only make the walk a couple times because I'm bleeding too much. At this rate, I'll use up my stockpile in less than a week.

* * *

The next day, I test Grendel by taking him out of the cave. He'll either survive the swim with me or he'll die. He can't remain in the cave forever, so together, we have no choice.

I have him in my arms when I jump into the mere. Not wanting to risk any seconds to see if he's okay, I just hurry under the wall and emerge quickly on the other side, holding him up so he can breathe the air. I expect him to be choking and gasping, but instead he's waving his arms and legs as if excited. He was surrounded in water before his birth and now he's returned to it.

Rather than venturing out of the mere, I return back to the cave. Once again, Grendel reacts with glee rather than displeasure. I'm relieved to know he'll be okay as we move in and out of the cave.

* * *

After two weeks, the bleeding hasn't stopped. I think about all the herbs I didn't take from ma's garden and realize the one she used to pick just before going to attend a village birth is one I didn't retrieve. I don't know what that herb in particular does, but it must have some secret remedy for a new mother. Even though I got to observe most births, I didn't get to help much, so I was still learning some of those herbs and how they were used. Right now, I wished I had learned more.

I have no choice but to retrieve it. As much as I don't want to take Grendel with me all that distance, again, I have no choice.

We have begun to find our routine.

Upon waking, I jump into the water, cleaning myself as much as I can, using new moss, feed Grendel while breakfasting, then leave him on the furs while I retrieve wood from the dragon's doorway. By the time I am finished, Grendel nurses again and then sleeps. That's when I take short excursions out of the cave, but not where I go hunting. Instead, I gather any food I can find nearby. One time I find the dead carcass of a bird. I bring it back and cook it as a soup, a tasty change from smoked meat and stored roots.

During the rest of the day, in between feeding Grendel, I work on the furs or bones, making utensils and tools. The furs, I scrape clean and then dry them for blankets or coverings. It is useless to make clothes as I once knew them. Instead, all I need is a wrap or a long covering that has a hole in the middle for my head that I use for cave wear, but such a wrap is awkward for nursing. With one fur, I end up creating a special covering for me that is more like a cape, big enough I can wrap it around me if needed, but leaving my front exposed for nursing while walking. The cape hangs to just below my knees. I don't want to be encumbered by it but need enough hide to huddle within it when I crouch down and wait while hunting. The fur allows me to blend into the landscape, while staying covered from the weather and any nuisance bugs or other tiny creatures.

I consider using ma's blanket for my next project, but it's not weather proof and wouldn't repel water like fur. So, with another piece of fur, I make a separate blanket, large enough to cradle and carry Grendel for some time, yet allow him the ability to nurse while in it. I make holes on each end, big enough for my head. I try putting Grendel in it, but there is no way to keep him from falling out of one end or the other. I experiment putting one hole over my head, and then the other through an arm and shoulder but with him in it. The shoulder end slips down, with Grendel sliding out of it, nearly falling to the floor.

It takes nearly two days and many tries before I find a satisfying solution, having started over with a second skin. This one ends up as a combination sling and pouch. With it on, half of my torso is covered when he is nursing. If I need more cover for the both of us, I can grab the side of my cape and tuck it into the pouch, under or around Grendel's feet. The weather will have to be especially cold for me to cover myself that way. Between Grendel's fur and the cape around my shoulders and backside, I'm not used to all that warmth. I can only imagine how it looks when carrying Grendel. Half of my body covered in fur, the other half partially naked with tiny feet appearing to stick out of my furry chest, and with a heavily lopsided body.

As long as I can carry Grendel in relative safety, allowing him access to my breasts or sleep, he can be satisfied as I travel, and I am happy in my own comfort, able to shift the sling to the other side when needed with ease. As much as I want to take the sling and cape outside to hide them away, they won't dry properly in this cold. The furs will repel the water quickly enough, and my body heat, if I wrap us up tightly right away when we first get out of the water, will warm us quickly and efficiently. When we return for our first venture out, I can then store the furs outside for future trips. But for this first trip, we'll have to make do.

I'm determined it'll work.

I halt in my chore and realize this is the first time I've considered us as a team. I look at this tiny sleeping baby with his large head and not-so-normal limbs and wonder how long we'll survive. His face no longer looks funny to me. With his flattened nose, he even snorts a bit when nursing, and my heart melts as I watch him every time. It's no miracle we've made it this far. It's taken hard work and planning, but we can do it. I can do it.

* * *

We start out the next day, mid-day. Once we come out of the water, I am relieved that the colder air from the day before is gone, but it is wet and still a bit chilly. I'm happy to see that Grendel appears unaffected by either the wet or cold. I grab the robe I have already hidden and wrap it around us, hoping it will warm us up quickly, and it does.

Once we're reasonably dry after walking a bit, I stash the second robe. I'll retrieve it on the way home.

Halfway to the village, I stop to switch the sling to the other side. I wake Grendel up doing so, but I'd rather he be awake now than later on when we are close to the village.

The extra exercise today is making me bleed more than usual. There is nothing I can do about the blood that oozes down my legs. From time to time, I stop and wipe as much off as I can, but I don't like that I smell like a wounded animal to other prey out here in the woods. I'm terrified that a bear or even a wolf could be tracking us.

I pay special attention to all of my senses as we travel through the forest. I'm probably being overly sensitive, but if I become complacent, that's when it becomes most dangerous for us. I don't like it when a breeze swirls around us, masking sounds, and confusing my sense of smell. When the breezes occur, all I can do is to stand still and wait for the air to become calm again before moving forward. The last thing I want to do is walk into a trap—whether animal or man's.

Dark comes early, and I'm glad. I am glad, too, for the nearly full moon. I know the moon can make my traveling more dangerous, but I need to be able to see in the distance. As I get closer to the village, I will be able to detect movement from others better. Also, I will need to be able to see the individual plants in the garden.

At the rocks where I hid months earlier, I decide to leave Grendel. He's sleeping and I can move more quickly without him.

Cautiously, I move into the garden and gather what I need. I stuff the desired leaves in the pocket I created inside the robe. No one is the wiser. Only when I am retrieving Grendel, do I realize that I did not sweep out my footprints with fallen brush.

Grendel moves, making motions like he is waking up. Too late. There is nothing I can do about it now, not unless I go back into the garden with him. It's my only option and I'm not sure if I should.

Quickly, I get him situated in the sling, fumbling with my breast as I move. He latches on. I start moving out of there. Due to my excursion, I don't wrap the cape around me. I want to feel the cool air on my skin. I look back to make sure we haven't been seen. Relieved, I come around the last of the big rock, only to be confronted by two men.

Startled, I yell.

They yell, too. Not men. Boys. They fall back, tripping over themselves and fall on the ground.

Grendel becomes unattached and starts screaming, his legs exposed, kicking at my chest.

I charge at the boys, growling.

They cower, covering their heads with their hands, screaming, "Monster! Monster!"

Suddenly, I hear voices behind me. Villagers are coming out of their houses.

I turn and run, not caring that Grendel is screaming. I run until I can't run anymore. I stop, reposition Grendel, quieting him. He stops crying and suckles. I listen to hear if anyone follows me. I hear nothing. But, I can't take any chances. We can't return to the cave by the direct route tonight. I'll have to go in another direction in the event someone decides to follow us later tonight or tomorrow. Fortunately, I can still retrieve the other fur.

If I know anything about these people, they'll huddle around the fire demanding the two boys retell their story, determining if any new information about their experience is forthcoming. What will they say? Surely, they won't recognize me. Hopefully not. I didn't recognize them. Nor will they venture out in the middle of the night looking for . . . a monster. Me.

I've become something for men to hunt, to talk about around the campfire. Or will the men convince the boys that I was a bear or their imagination? With Grendel's feet flailing at my chest, I'll probably be some two-head monster, half human, half animal, who eats babies or some such nonsense.

For the first time in a long time, I am smiling.

* * *

Before we're too close to the cave and I climb a familiar tree, keeping Grendel with me, so that I have a better view. I'm surprised how much stronger I am now than I was months ago when I once slept in this tree. I notice, too, that I don't have to stretch to reach the branches as I climb higher. Have I grown a few inches since being out here?

Frankly, I'm glad that I have become stronger. I feel better knowing I can defend myself. That I made two boys piss all over themselves last night. I chuckle at the thought. I would have liked being at that campfire hearing their tales. They probably made me out to be far taller and bigger than I am.

I stay in the tree for about an hour. Not seeing anything out of the ordinary, I decide it is safe enough to return home. Once I'm back on the ground, it starts raining. I'm glad, for that means my footprints will be washed away.

There will be no tracking this monster, not this day.

* * *

Back home, I get the fire going hot, placing a few of the leaves I picked earlier into a pot to boil for tea. By the time the tea is ready, Grendel is dry and settled, sleeping soundly. Thinking back on this recent event, I'm astonished at how I didn't panic. I didn't think. Instead, I just reacted. My skills have grown. So, has my confidence. I look at Grendel. Could he be responsible for this shift in my thinking? Or is it because I've been here on my own for so long now that I didn't realize how confident I have become?

* * *

Before Grendel's birth, I was somewhat careful what I threw into the mere discovering whatever I threw into the cave water ended up in the outside portion of the mere; but as Grendel grows, he has no compunction; he ignores me and throws everything and anything into the pool. Sometimes, I think he does so blatantly, just to antagonize me. As a result, the water has become quite disgusting, and all the animals avoid it. Except for the eels or the fire snakes, as Grendel calls them. The snakes arrived as blood began accumulating in the mere due to my kills that I was gutting in the cave. It's why I didn't worry about jumping into the mere after Grendel's birth.

Previously, I had seen the eels only once in my lifetime and that was when da had brought them home from a hunting. I don't remember where he fished them, but they were quite tasty, as I recall.

Once the eels arrived in the mere, I noticed the water became clearer, less red. The algae, however, remains the same.

Truthfully, I have to admit that the snakes provide an extra layer of security for us as no one who happens upon the mere will be compelled to dive in to cool off or to look for fish. Since we have to move through this water to exit the cave, I no longer consider how we must smell or even appear. To me, it's normal. I stopped looking at my image in the waters long ago. What does it matter how I look?

We have become part of the forest, part of the landscape that provides, nurtures, and secures our safety and endurance.

I let go of that girl I once was and live in complete freedom, better than any freedom I thought existed.

* * *

These first years are not easy as I care of Grendel. He's grown into an inquisitive youngster having been an extremely inquisitive baby. The questions never stop. I wonder if he gets that curious nature from me.

He likes to hide and watch me panic as I try to find him. He only tried to go into the dragon's tunnel one time. That venture scared him good, and I punished him further at the time, by keeping him in the cave for two whole days. He loves the outdoors even more than I. He's obsessed with the outdoors, in fact.

Right now, he's still a youngster and can't go far, but I fear for that day when he'll have more energy, discovers the bigger world outhere, and begins to challenge me. Already, he comes up to my waist. I have only a few years left to influence him.

* * *

I feel I have failed. By the time Grendel is five, he dives in and out of the cave at will. For a while, I was able to keep him close to the mere, always within shouting distance. Our signal for each other became a wolf's howl at night and an owl's hoot by day. Our howls and hoots were just enough different from the real that we knew each other's calls from the animals themselves. I could only hope that ours were close enough to the real thing that hunters and anyone else who might traverse this area wouldn't suspect a thing.

Our tracks, though, I can't do anything about. I taught Grendel how to avoid any ground that would lay an impression of his print, but as I watch him in the woods, he is more often careless than careful.

I do what I can when we are outside, teaching him my skills, hunting together, learning new skills together. He's a clever boy, too clever. Too inquisitive for his own good.

This night I am outside and come up behind him as he stands at the mere's edge. I see him toss a bone into the water. Purposely, I step on a twig. It snaps. He turns, growling. He's covered in blood from head to toe, and with dirt as another layer. He tells me he found a wolf's den with four tiny pups in it. When I ask if he has been in the den he says no, but his appearance tells me not to believe him. I don't want to doubt him, but how can I tell if he's telling the truth? I don't know if I want to hear how he handled the pups, let alone killed them.

I've seen how he enjoys killing spiders, pulling their legs off one-by-one, watching them squirm and twist on the one leg he holds them by, before he eats it. In fact, he eats all bugs with relish. As much as I've told him we should respect Nature and her creatures, he tells me he's hungry and they're for eating, just like the deer and pigs that I kill.

How can I argue with that?

The next morning, he tells me he twisted their little bodies, leaving them in the den.

He laughs, then tells me he ate them.

I am disgusted by what I hear. How could I have failed him have failed so badly?

When I ask him why he did it, he tells me he wanted to see how soft they were. I know from my own brothers how curious little boys can be, but were any of those boys destructive, like Grendel?

These first few years I was protective and still am. I try to teach him to care for Nature. In doing so, I try to convince him that She will in turn care for us. He laughs at me.

As Grendel continues to grow, he becomes stronger, more curious, more independent, and at the same time disobedient because of that curiosity. There isn't much I do, especially when he scampers out of my reach and I'm unable to locate him for hours at a time

I continue to educate, but that education goes in one ear and out the other. Grendel insists that he needs to experience everything firsthand and goes out into the world despite my protests. Like a curious bear cub or chipmunk that doesn't observe and that results in their death, I fear this child is destined to die early or be caught. He has no patience, is quick to react. Like both my father and my mother, he wants to best everyone. I don't see that trait as flattering. Was it my trait, too? Is it still?

I've grown used to his distorted face, which looks more animal than human, and he's learned to compensate for his shorter arm extremely well. His leg is less twisted and his speed belies any handicap. If I didn't know better, I would say he has no handicap.

* * *

Now that's he's almost ten, his head is far bigger than his body. His head is bony with ridges and strange bumps. I notice that he walks with his upper torso more forward than his lower extremities. I wonder if his skin is okay because he won't let me touch him anymore. He claims it hurts when I touch him. Even bent over slightly, he's already taller than me. How much bigger will he get?

I'm in the cave, adding wood to the coals to smoke my earlier kill, to start adding to the larder for winter.

Lately, Grendel has taken to leaving the cave before I'm awake and not returning until it is nearly dark out. As much as I ask, he doesn't reveal where he goes, other than to say that he's learning. Once in a while, he brings home food, but those times are becoming rare.

Hours later, long after dark has descended, Grendel comes in and tosses down a pig. Only it's not a wild pig. It's a domesticated pig.

"Where did you find this?"

"In the woods." He grabs a knife and goes back to the pig, which he left by the pond's edge.

"Where in the woods?"

"A place we've never been before. I doubt you've been there either." He stabs the knife in the belly and slits it open. Its innards fall into mere.

"Wait! We could have used—"

"I don't like organs!"

I know better than to continue to argue. He'll either become louder or violent, possibly both. Finally, I ask, "You haven't been to the village, have you?"

"No. You told me not to go there." He rinses the knife off in the mere and walks away from the pig.

He expects me to wash it out and skin it.

"Another village?" I ask, keeping my voice low.

"So what?"

I refrain from saying anything. I wash the pig, letting my gaze fall on the pig rather than on him, but I am watching him out of the corner of my eye. He's frowning. He's curious why I'm not saying anything.

"I don't like how men treat me!" he bursts out.

I'm horrified. What men? Where? When? I try to refrain from letting my anxiety seep into my actions or my tone of voice. "They didn't treat you well?"

"No, I wanted to talk and ask questions about a contraption they were using in the field, but they yelled at me. Threw rocks. When they weren't looking, I went back and took their pig."

Once I have cut off a leg and a huge hunk of meat, I get up and take it to Grendel, who is at the fire, poking a stick in the coals. He takes it, immediately biting into it. I go back to the pig and begin processing it.

He takes a few bites, chewing thoughtfully. Finally, he says, "What's your name?"

I stop and sit back on my heels. "What?" I'm glad my back is to him and that he can't see my face.

"Everyone has a name. My name is Grendel. I hear people call out to each other with names."

"What people?"

"In the village."

"What village? I don't want you going—"

"You can't stop me! It's not your village anyway. It's a different one."

"It's still dangerous!"

"I know you have a name!"

"It's forgotten."

"Not by me. I'll remember it always."

"Stay away from other people. They'll hurt you."

"Your name is important."

"Not anymore."

"I'll remember it."

"You haven't heard it."

"Tell me."

"No."

"What can I call you, then?"

"What you've always called me. Mother."

I never want my name spoken ever again. Until now, I never thought about never hearing my name spoken. I wasn't that young girl anymore. And, I would never be her again.

Suddenly, I feel old.

* * *

The winter passes. Spring is upon us. Grendel leaves every day and returns every night. From time to time, he brings home a sword. A helmet. The pile of paraphernalia grows. I begin to worry for that time when he will choose not to come home. Do I say anything now or wait until that time? Will I get to have a say?

I exit the cave and the mere. Grendel exits the forest and walks toward me, one hand behind his back. I wait. What surprise is upon me?

He stops in front. With a big smile, a lopsided smile, his arm comes around. He holds a bouquet of dandelions, some new, some barely open, others fully open, and a few already gone to seed. He knows how much I like this flower. I'm touched that he's thought of me.

I take the flowers. He inhales deeply and blows on them.

I gasp. I'm surprised.

He's never done that before.

That long-ago memory of ma's words and then later a monster blowing the seeds to the wind flit into my thoughts.

Quickly, I dismiss them.

I shudder.

Grendel frowns. "You don't like them?"

"No, I do like them," I say. I smile at him.

He grins widely. If only he could remain this little boy. This gentle giant in front of me who is a head taller than me.

* * *

I come home and find Grendel in front of the fire, his back to me as I emerge from the mere.

He doesn't turn around as is his normal habit.

Only when I am behind him do I see why.

He has taken the sword off the wall, and it lies in front of him. He fondles it, stroking its length.

"That's not yours." My voice startles him.

He continues stroking and fondling. "None of them are."

"Put it back."

"No."

I pause in telling him what to do, knowing I have no control over him the way I used to. I do the only thing I can to scare him. "Then deal with the dragon."

He twists around, his eyes wide. He's both curious and fearful.

"The dragon? This is Hers?"

"Yes."

"For real?"

"Yes."

His one encounter with the dragon when he was about two, close to three years old, scared him. The only time I've ever seen him scared.

I was at the fire stirring broth in a pot and he wandered off, apparently down to the dragon's lair, I soon discovered. I never heard him leave my side. I heard the roar, though. I could tell by the roar that she had breathed fire.

Grendel burst into our part of the cave screaming, his hair singed. He howled. It took some time before he settled down and told me that he had thrown rocks at what he thought was a rock with an eye watching him.

He claimed he would never go back there again, and he never has. Not even to help me with moving firewood.

Grendel rises, bends over to pick up the sword. He howls and drops it. The noise amplifies and echoes against the walls. "It bit me!"

He holds out his hand. He's been cut.

"It's not a toy. Handle it with respect."

I refuse to coddle him like he wants. He glares at me, though I know he's really glaring at the sword. Gingerly, he picks it up and returns it back to its shelf. Not as far back as I'd prefer but where an edge of the hilt is still visible.

"It hurts," he whines. He sucks at the weeping blood.

"It should." I want to say more, but don't.

When I look up at the shelf again, I suddenly see death.

I shake the image away.

Of course, I would see death. It's a sword. It's an instrument meant to kill.

As much as I want the image gone from my mind's eye, it stays with me throughout the day. I'm not willing to see the image to its end to discover whose death.

I don't want to know.

* * *

Not too long soon after that discussion, Grendel begins to stay out all night. He can be gone for days at a time. I panic the first time, not able to sleep until he is home safe.

I worry about him constantly. When he does come home, he barks at me, telling me to stop badgering him. He laughs, learning I'm up all night, waiting for him.

I try my best to protect him, to help him see reason as to why we need to keep to ourselves, but he argues with me.

* * *

Years pass and it's impossible for me to say anything. He's taller than me, taller than anyone I've ever known. Probably as tall as his father, I daresay. Worse, he's mean and temperamental.

He tells me his head hurts all the time, and that the only relief he can find is when he's in the forest at night, howling with the other animals. His face, most definitely resembles that of an animal, cat like almost, but not a cat I've ever seen.

He's able to bring down a healthy tree, about twice his height, merely by pushing on it. We actually have some furniture in the cave— even if a couple simple benches and a table—because of Grendel. He told me he had looked through the windows of homes where men lived and saw the furniture, wondering why we had none. That was the only time Grendel took an interest in any of our tools, creating something for our home. The furniture is rough, even wobbly. He never accepts any advice from me, always cutting me off, silencing me. He has to learn it himself, he says. So reluctantly, I leave him alone.

We have bear more frequently, now, too. A couple years ago, when we were out hunting, I had wounded a bear with my spear but not killed him, and the bear began charging at me. Grendel jumped in front of me, growled at the bear, knocking the bear on its side when it tried to claw at Grendel. I watched a boy, I had seen as sweet, but still a boy, become a man that day. With a growling grimace, he grabbed the bear's jaw and the top of its head, snapping the bear's neck with a solid crack. Grendel was puffed with pride at his achievement. Granted, I welcomed the fur, the fat, and the meat we got from the bear, but I suddenly realized that my son could be a powerful enemy, and he was still a teenager, at the time.

I've learned that he visits Hrothgar's mead hall regularly. Far too frequently, in my mind. He tells me how he sneaks into the hall where the thanes sleep and plays tricks on them—taking their weapons and placing them in a pile outside the door, but wedging the door so they can't get out when he howls, waking them up. It's his favorite stunt, and one he likes to repeat from time to time. On cold nights when water freezes, he pours water on the steps and pathway leading up to the hall, using their buckets, and then watches from a distance the next morning as the men slide on the thin ice, falling on their butts or backs. It's hilarious, he tells me.

I see it all as dangerous.

I can't convince him to stay away. He hates being bored and is only playing with them, so he tells me. It isn't like he wants to hurt them.

Why is it I believe he's not telling the truth?

* * *

When storms come through and he's in the cave, he holds his large head in his hands and wails. I've learned I can soothe some of his pain with strong herbal tea, literally drugging him, but by morning, I always find him gone, having disappeared in the night.

I'm beginning to see more and more men in areas of the forest where I never used to see them before. Fortunately, I always see them before they see me. Once in a while, I hear snippets of their conversation.

I fear they may be hunting my son.

* * *

Today, Grendel hasn't returned as normal. As is his nature. The longest he's ever been gone is three days, but now it's been five. Yesterday and today, I leave the cave to sit near the mere or climb a nearby tree, to see if I can detect him anywhere in the nearby forest, but his movements are good. I see no sign of him. I've taught him well. I contemplate where to go to see if I can pick up a trail. As I start to climb down the tree, he runs out of the forest, his furs red with blood. He dives into the mere, and the blood spreads throughout the water. The eels start churning up the water as they eat the blood.

I scamper down the tree and dive in the mere, following him. He's devouring a leg of a ram that he killed the other day, a ram he claims that battled him several years ago and bested him. When Grendel dropped the ram at my feet that day, he boastfully asked, "Who's the better hunter now?"

"Where have you been?" I ask.

"Out."

"Your furs were red."

"They always are."

Fear crawls along my skin. This game of his isn't play anymore.

"Don't say it, Mother."

"Say what?"

"That what I'm doing isn't safe."

"You already know that."

"Good. We're in agreement." He throws the bone on the fire and climbs into his sleeping furs. I retrieve the bone from the fire. I can use another mallet.

I sit at the fire, wondering and worrying about his future.

I fear one day he won't come back, and then I'll be alone once again. I don't know if I can endure that day to come.

Then, I realize. . . I already am alone. That day is here. I'm alone more days than not. And generally, when he is here, he's asleep or too grumpy for me to want to be around him. How long will he tolerate my presence before he wants to leave this area and find a mate?

But, what woman will have him?

None that I can think of.

His size alone will frighten any woman, let alone a girl. Was I raped for that very reason?

I've never seen him cuddle any creature, not even with me when he was little. Once he no longer got to nurse, he rejected me, pushing me away anytime I tried to hug him. At the time, I thought he was just being a boy, just like my brothers used to be, but now I have to wonder if there's something different about him beyond his size and his looks.

The next morning, I try again by asking him about this hall he's been spying on.

"Heorot Hall."

"King Hrothgar's mead hall?"

"You know it?"

"He began building just before you were born. Hrothgar will protect it."

Grendel snorts. "Not so far."

"Stay away from it."

"Don't tell me what to do, Mother. Stop nagging. Stop or I won't come back."

He runs to the mere.

I shout after him, "You'll be—"

He dives into the water and is gone.

"—back." I've chased him away.

No, he chose to leave. I only want what is best for him, to keep him safe and from harm. Taunting Hrothgar's men will come to no good.

* * *

Grendel doesn't come home for three days. Then, it becomes five days. By the seventh day, I wonder if he is following through with his threat of not coming back.

I can't stand it any longer. I have to go look for him. It takes me a full day to make my way to Hrothgar's hall, and I arrive late at night. I climb a tree quite a ways away, for my own safety. From here, at this height, I have a better view through the windows.

As the evening wears on, the mead flows in the hall. I see no sign of Grendel. I relax, but then I hear the loud boasts of catching a monster. Are they talking about Grendel? As I strain to listen, I hear them repeat the stories Grendel has told me. And then, I hear Hrothgar announce that he has fifteen men coming to find this monster on his command.

I don't wait to hear anymore. I climb down and leave quietly, without anyone the wiser of my visit.

I need to find Grendel and warn him.

I bypass the last village before the mere, my old village, taking a wide path so as not to meet anyone else, when I begin hearing something whimpering, almost as if trapped or suffering. I follow the sound, careful not to reveal my presence.

I squat down, waiting to hear more. And then, I hear talking. Grendel! But, who is he talking with?

I'm cautious.

I don't want to walk into a trap and find Grendel has been captured and talking to his captures.

I wait and listen.

No, it's only Grendel's voice.

He's talking to himself, much like he used to do when he was a small boy.

But, I can't see him. Something is different here.

Carefully, I move forward, but slowly.

I'm glad I did, for about a dozen steps in front of me is a deep muddy drop off, with no way up the sides. Deep, with no exits or entrances, I've found a number of these holes in my travels, but never one this big. It's almost as if the earth has opened up. I wonder why I never saw this one before. Is it new?

I go to the edge and hunker down. "Grendel," I whisper.

He shouts. "Get me out of here!" The sound echoes.

I tell him to be quiet.

I find a length of a tree limb and toss it into the hole. Grendel is able to climb up the limb until he can grab the vine I found and dangle in front of him. I hold on tight, with it wrapped around a tree for leverage, as he climbs out. Once he's out, I toss the vine into the hole.

Immediately, I start walking home, expecting him to follow. He does. But, the walk isn't silent. He rants about how someone set out to trap him. I try to tell him that it's a natural formation and that he should be grateful that I saved him rather than Hrothgar's army.

"Hrothgar has no army," he boasts.

"Fifteen men are coming and they're coming to hunt a monster."

"A monster?"

"You!" I turn around and face him, furious at his stupidity. I pound the sides of my fists on his stomach and chest. He grabs my arms and pushes me back. I nearly stumble. "Don't you get it?" I yell at him, "You're their monster!"

I turn and stomp through the forest unable to say another word, mad at myself for screaming, putting both of us in danger.

* * *

My words mean nothing. Life continues, unchanged. Grendel stays angry, stubborn, and now haughty. I worry. When he does come home, I nag. I plead. But, I refuse to cry tears. To me, tears are a weakness. When it comes to Grendel, I can't afford to be weak.

I hunt, as usual, but I'm more cautious now. Thanks to Grendel, men could be in my woods. I cook, but I'm only cooking for myself. Grendel doesn't eat in the cave anymore. Now and then I find a bone or two near the mere. Rather than leave them, I always bring them into the cave. I don't want to provide anyone a reason to believe that anyone is living near here. From time-to-time, I do a sweep of branches to eliminate our footprints. Grendel tells me that I'm paranoid. Maybe so, but I refuse to let his foolish ways lead me into danger.

I begin to wonder what worth I have if I cannot raise Grendel into becoming a caring person. Where did I fail him?

As I ponder the situation, I wonder if my parents felt this way about me. No, they never would have thought that they failed me. They believed I failed them, which is why they sacrificed me to the dragon.

Should I blame Grendel, making him responsible for our plight? For his not taking responsibility for his behavior?

What value do I have as his mother anymore?

* * *

Grendel has been gone for a week, again. Just as I was getting up to start the day, he returns.

He's exuberant, unable to sit still. He pushes away my offer of food, telling me he's too excited to eat.

I don't want to ask. I'm not sure I want to know. He tells me anyway.

"I killed thirty of Hrothgar's men last night." He dances around the fire. "While they were sleeping! No one can catch me. Look at me! Not a single scratch!" He laughs and makes fun of the men, mimicking their horror, their cries, their dismay.

I don't like what I'm seeing. This isn't the son I raised. Ever since he started leaving the cave on his own, I have watched him come and go. I dislike his lack of fear and his pride of killing innocent men.

I've grown weary of that pride. I fear for his life.

Suddenly, I remember the dandelion, the one with blown seeds. The seeds he blew in my face. Has he set us on a path of danger? To death? It certainly appears so.

* * *

In the ensuing days and nights, Grendel comes home, boasting of how Hrothgar's men are trying to find him. Grendel speaks with glee, telling me that he is often high in a tree, watching the men, like ants on the ground, unable to track him. They're so stupid, he says, befuddled when his tracks vanish. "Not once do they look up! So stupid!" Grendel laughs. I come to know that laugh. It is his acknowledgment that he is superior and that they will never catch him.

I can only wish it to be true. If a king has sent away for men from another land, though, my son is living a fool's paradise.

* * *

Grendel comes home, telling me that a soldier named Beowulf has arrived, a warrior who boasts of many battles. When I learn that Grendel attacked the hall, taking one of Beowulf's men, killing him, separating his head from his body, and leaving the body where Beowulf and King Hrothgar would find it easily enough, I plead with Grendel.

"Stop. Please stop. This game of yours has to end."

Grendel turns on me. For the first time, I want to cower. But, I stand tall and refuse to back down.

"Leave it, Mother. No more." He spins around and dives into the mere.

I let out a huge sigh of disappointment. There's nothing that I can do. Yet, I can't just give up.

* * *

I give him a day before I consider searching for him. On the second day, I sense something is horribly wrong.

I can't sit here waiting for his return anymore. Knowing that Hrothgar has sent for warriors, I'm more worried than ever before. I'm anxious knowing Grendel's temper drives him and sets him off. He thinks he's invincible. I need to know that he's safe.

I decide to make my way to Hrothgar's hall. I doubt myself while walking. I procrastinate going there by checking Grendel's favorite haunts. I wish him into one of these places, site after site. In my heart, I know where he is—Hrothgar's hall.

The thought of returning to an area that is trampled by men fills me with dread. I head in that direction, anyway. I get as far as my old village. I circle around the village, the place I once called home, noting the disrepair, how some homes look deserted, with smoke escaping from only a few of the chimneys.

I hesitate. It's daylight and Grendel likes to attack in the dark. He wouldn't be there now. Would he?

I hunt the forest for any clue, but there are no footprints, no sign of disturbance other than the creatures that inhabit the woods, streams, and fields. Where is he? Am I just an over-protective, anxious mother of a boy turning man?

I decide, instead, to go to the cave and wait. If he hasn't returned tomorrow, I'll go to the hall, then.

At the mere, I take one last look around before diving into the water and moving automatically under the rock.

The minute my head surfaces the water in the cave, I see Grendel lying before the fire, his back to me. I hear him groaning. Quickly, I go to him and turn him onto his back. He groans loudly and clutches his shoulder. His arm is gone!

Blood spills thickly between his fingers, spreading out on the floor.

I grab furs, anything that I can press against the gaping wound. He's so pale. Hardly able to speak, I lift his head and give him sips of water.

"You were right," he sputters. "I shouldn't have—"

"Shhh, don't talk."

"Beowulf. . . my arm."

He dies in my arms. I can't save him. There is nothing I can do. For the first time in years, I cry. His blood spilled all that distance.

I moan and rock him like I did when he was a baby. I lose track of time. For the first time, the fire goes out. I don't care anymore.

I can't bring myself to bury him, so I move the food supplies out of the little room and pull Grendel into it. I want my boy safe, where no one can harm him anymore. I want to know where he is.

I need fire. I have no choice but to go to the dragon. She cautions me to stay away from Hrothgar's hall or I'll suffer the same fate. I tell her I have no desire to fight anyone. I'm too tired.

The next morning, I hear what sounds like thunder, but it's not thunder I've ever heard before. I recognize the sound from my girlhood days—horses. Lots of them. They're looking for Grendel. Eventually, the sound drifts away. They can't find him. They'll never find him, I determine. I'll make sure of that.

My anger builds. An anger I've never felt, not even when I was raped, when I was rejected by the community, my parents, or even when I was rejected by Erik. This anger is hot, white-hot, like coals in the fire when the flames burned blue.

I want to know what happened.

That night finds me at the windows of the mead hall. I'm stunned. My son's arm hangs from the rafters. Beneath it, men guzzle their ale, celebrating as if it were a trophy.

And then I notice, the celebration is a banquet honoring Beowulf.

He doesn't look so great a warrior to me. Yes, he is a little taller than all the other men and has plenty of muscle under his armor, but he is still a man.

And men bleed. All of them.

He boasts more than the others. Claims he killed the monster. My son. Grendel wasn't perfect, but he was still mine. The longer I remain, the angrier I become.

I want revenge for my son's death, but I'm not ready. I need to be strong.

In time.

* * *

The winter weather is harsh. Colder than normal. I spend my time hunting, pretending every throw of my spear sinks into Beowulf's belly rather than that of the animal that will give me strength to endure.

My need for revenge grows.

Every day, I walk to the forest next to Hrothgar's hall. Quickly, I learn where the men like to hunt and the lands they avoid, which are the lands that I inhabit naturally. Actually, I prefer them as I can hide easily in the mud, the mushy landscape that nourishes the rushes and tall grasses. At first, because I spook the wildlife that live in these landscapes around the great hall, the animals end up on tips of men's spears. After a while, though, the wildlife accommodates my presence. They don't see me as a threat and don't run from me anymore.

I spy on the men's comings and goings, keeping track of who are the hunters, who are the slackers, who are the doers but never leave camp. These are the men who build spears, sharpen the knives and swords, make bows and arrows. All through their work, boasts are tossed about like fall's loose leaves in the breeze. Lots of sputter and pride but no substance behind the words. When challenged, the words crumble like dry leaves. Hoots and hollers follow the dismissal of their words.

I find their routine. I can see why Grendel would strike the hall at night. All the thanes are housed there, sleeping, at night. They don't even leave anyone on watch. They're stupid in their secure thoughts.

I wait until the crescent moon is high in the sky. I want the thanes asleep. I want to scare them. Shock them. Rattle their smug thoughts. Hear their hearts beating out of their chest.

I want them afraid.

Carefully, I open the door. I know how fast I can open it and how far before it begins to squeak. I've listened as they've entered and exited all these days.

Carefully, I step deep into the hall and climb on a table, again careful not to make a sound. I reach for Grendel's arm, nailed high on one of the structural beams that run across the entire width of the hall. I use a sword to pry to nail. Finally, the deed is done. I hug my son's severed arm to me.

In my haste to get out, I trip on a thane. He yells.

Suddenly, I'm trapped, close to the door, my back against a wall. I grab the closest thane, my arm around his neck, my hand still clutching Grendel's arm, the severed shoulder in his face.

He sputters, thrashing.

I grip him tighter and have my knife in my other hand, at his eye. The others back off.

I escape out the door, dragging the soldier with me. Quickly, I'm in the forest.

I hear their cries to Beowulf. The thane I hold cries out too. I slit his throat just enough to show I mean it. He stops struggling.

Hidden now and out of view of the thanes who pour out of the hall, I see a man running from one of the village houses to the great hall. The mighty Beowulf.

The men point to the forest, but Beowulf moves into the hall and the men follow. I hear the uproar that I'd taken their trophy.

I consider my options. I can't travel quickly with this man. He'll hinder me all the way. Not far into the forest, a bear rises, blocking the path. It growls, the ground quaking as he steps forward. I grab the thane's sword and swing hard. I miss the bear and behead the thane in the process.

Quickly, the bear grabs the body and runs off.

Angry that I have no prisoner, I drop the sword, pick up the man's head in one hand and Grendel's arm in the other.

I didn't want any trouble, but it seems when it comes to Grendel, trouble follows.

Nearly at the mere, I leave the head on a rock that overlooks the mere. Later, I would wonder why I didn't pitch it into the forest. Somewhere. Anywhere.

At the moment, I'm not thinking. I didn't even realize I was still holding it until I'm at the rocks where I hide my cloak.

I just know I don't want it in the cave.

* * *

Days later, I hear that strange thunder, the one of many horses. I hear shouting. The water ripples. The fire dragons are active.

Suddenly, I hear a scream unlike any heard before, only the scream comes from the water and fills the cave with its echoes. It is the snakes who scream. A stranger is in their waters.

I hear him before I see him. Beowulf. The mighty warrior. The braggart.

He climbs out of the water, wet and disheveled. This is no mighty warrior. This is a man, a mere man. Strong? Yes. Powerful? In his mind. Because he believes in his power, others believe in it, too.

I can kill him in the time it takes his eyes to adjust to the dim light, the fire just mere coals. I could have but I don't. I wonder why. Is it because he reminds me of Erik and that long-ago time when I thought him strong? Or, is it the dandelion I see stuck in his finely made, mail shirt?

Why couldn't Erik have stood by me? Loved me and protected me? Believed in me? We promised each other that we'd be each other's first and last. I never had that chance. My first was stolen from me, taken against my will, and now there would never be a last. All this time, I realize that I love Erik still.

No, I loved the memory, even though I tried to bury it, locking love away in my heart, never able to give the key to another. I loved you, but you turned your back on me. I am alone. Totally and utterly alone.

And now, here before me is the killer of my only child, the only child society will allow me.

My fury is full. Beowulf's sword is drawn. My advantage is gone.

With a roar, I race out of the shadows and bulldoze Beowulf before he knows what is happening, charging at him with my full body. He's forced backward and hits the wall, his sword in hand. His hard body bounces off the wall. He swings the sword and aims for my neck, but the sword doesn't bite into my skin.

I block his sword arm as he swings it back to gain momentum. He swings again, but weakly, and misses.

I jump back. I grab a sword, one of the many Grendel brought home.

Beowulf looks surprised. What did he expect? A monster?

I was a girl turned mother, a woman now, a warrior like him, turned angry.

It's not just about me anymore. He's fighting me, Grendel, and the dragon all rolled into one. Beowulf is outnumbered here. He invades my space, my territory. My family.

Beowulf is taller, by far. But his strength isn't any greater than mine. He fights with his sword. I fight mostly with my hands and my wit, but I have many swords, too.

We battle. He swings his sword; I swing mine, staying out of his way and he out of mine.

Coming at him from behind, I strike, stab, and surprise him. I'm faster. I can move freely. He's hindered with well-made threads of iron.

His sword strikes rock and breaks the iron in half.

Without a second's hesitation, he runs toward me, and at the last minute, jumps up in the air and lands on me, forcing me down. He pins my left shoulder to the ground and pain shoots down my left leg.

I get free and jump up, reaching for my small knife, lying on a rock shelf. I climb the rocks quickly and jump down on him, getting him in a stranglehold, my arm around his neck. He's surprised at my strength and fights back. I strike at his heart, but the iron threads protect him too well.

We wrestle for a long time, our strength and ability evenly matched.

Beowulf gives as good as he gets. Neither of us makes any deep cuts that give the other an advantage. I realize we can fight for hours more. Neither of us is tiring.

I attack. He defends. He attacks. I defend.

What do I hope to gain?

Yes, I can kill Beowulf, eventually. To what end?

I'll be hunted and pursued much like the village dogs who find a rat, gopher, or a squirrel. I'll be torn to shreds when found. Worse, I could be raped again. I never want to relive that experience. Ever.

I see him notice the wall. Where the giant sword lies.

Quickly, he scales the wall and grabs it. He jumps to the cave floor, swinging the sword. I hear it sing. Its power is now married to his.

Instinctively, I reach out to pick up a sword.

I hesitate.

I am no match for this newfound power. With that sword, we are no longer evenly matched.

My son is dead. These weeks have been too lonely. The winter too long. I can't continue this life, season after season. Everything I had is gone.

My desire to live drips from my soul like the blood dripping from the bone-deep slash on my arm. I have no desire to live anymore

I yearn to be free. Here, in this cave, I thought I was, but I'm not. Never was.

I wanted independence, control. Yes, I lived within Nature, but She was always in control.

Beowulf steps forward, the big sword raised high.

In death, I will be free.

I drop my arm, picking up nothing.

I smile.

He hesitates, his movement catching.

Then.

I hear the swoosh. He cuts off my head.

I feel no pain.

Suddenly, I'm looking down, from the ceiling.

I see blood pooling. My blood. See him bend over and pick up my head, claiming me as his. I see Beowulf dive into the mere with my head in his hand and hear the roar of his men when he emerges in the mere, outside of the cave.

I hear noise from the back of the cave that tells me the dragon has awoken. I recognize the slight sound of her wings that indicates flight. Hearing our battle, no doubt she's escaping and will have disappeared from the sky by the time Beowulf joins his men. Hopefully, his men will be watching the mere and not the sky, missing her disappearance. I hope she's able to escape far away from this land, and can find a new cave somewhere. She's afraid Beowulf will find her, that he'll investigate the cave and find her secret hideout. But now she's gone, never to return. I hope she's able to find respite, a safe haven, safer than even this one. If not, he'll destroy her, too.

No doubt Beowulf will take my head back to the mead hall and hang it up like a trophy, just like they did with Grendel's arm. They'll celebrate and drink merrily until they are in a stupor of drunkenness and stupidity.

The more I reflect on my past, the more I realize that I was never deeply engaged.

I went through the motions each day but did I love? Was I loved? Was I ever happy outside of Nature?

If I were to examine my life more closely, would it come apart like threads of a tapestry unsecured around the edges?

No, I knew love for a time, when Grendel first entered my life. Then, like a candle snuffed, so was he.

* * *

No doubt, Beowulf will claim me, in my death, as his. He lies. I let him kill me. I simply let go. I didn't want to fight anymore.

Not him. Not society. Not even life.

Beowulf thought he had put an end to me, but he is wrong. No man can claim me as his. I belong to death and eternal life. My body has no breath, but I live on, for I am Mother, one with Nature: wild and free, solidly within Her chaos that has structure.

I am Nature.

I endure.

I survive.

I am the warmth of the earth, the heat of the fire, the dandelion sun.

I am the dandelion.

Man will never be rid of me.

I take pleasure that the stake I had been chained to before the dragon rescued me is no more. Time stepped forward and Nature diminished the stake. A few remaining strands of wood are scattered about the ground, most buried and surrounded by a field of dandelions.

And me? I will always be Grendel's Mother.

About The Author

Diana Stout, MFA, Ph.D. is an award-winning screenwriter, author, and former English professor, whose writing led her into academic teaching. Her students would say, "She smiles when she talks about writing."

Published in multiple genres, her career began with magazine articles and short stories. She's a former magazine and newspaper columnist. She's served as a contest judge for screenwriting organizations, and writers' groups, and enjoys helping other writers learn the craft.

When not writing, she enjoys reading, watching movies, jigsaw puzzles, and the small town where she grew up.

Also by Diana Stout

Nonfiction
Finding Your Fire & Keeping It Hot
The Super Simple Easy Basic Cookbook
CPE: Characters, Plot, & Emotion
CPE Workbook

Epic Fantasy
Grendel's Mother

Romance
Determined Hearts
Love's New Beginnings
Tomorrow's Wish for Love

Laurel Ridge Novella Series
Laurel Ridge: Seven Ways to Love
Shattered Dreams #1
Burning Desire #2
Arrested Pleasures #3
Buried Hearts #4
Tangled Passions #5
Reserved Yearnings #6
Sweet Cravings #7

Literary / Short Story
Maggie's Story

Anthology / Collections
Lost and Found (story contribution & editor)
Unlock My Heart (story contribution)

Screenplays published as books
David & Goliath
Charlie's Christmas Carole

Follow Diana Stout

You can follow links to her social media from her website, Sharpened Pencils Productions: sharpenedpencilsproductions.com

Blogs

Behind the Scenes – life as a writer, dianastout.net

Into the Core – life as an intuitive, dianastout.com

Featured Guests with Diana Stout, dianastout.org

***

Can You Help?

Did you know that reviews are important? That readers rely on reviews when determining whether to read a story?

Reviews can be short, such as:
- I loved this book!
- These characters were wonderful.
- I couldn't put the book down!

It's not the length of a review that counts; it's the number of reviews that a book receives that engage the site's algorithms for advertising purposes.

Please consider leaving a review at any location where you buy or share books: Goodreads, Amazon, BookBub, etc.

THANK YOU!